Published by: Cornwall Writers

Text Design by: Tracey Dockree

Cover Design by: Ruta Ciutaite of Blue Rue Designs

ISBN: 978-1-8380932-0-4

Distributed by:

Cornwall Writers

Princes House

Princes Street

Truro

Cornwall TR1 3HZ

Cornwall Writers

Cornwall: Misfits, Curiosities and Legends

A Collection of Short Stories and other scribbles

Cornwall:

Misfits, Curiosities & Legends

A Collection of

Short Stories

Cornwall Writers

Acknowledgements

Red Pen editor, Anne Rainbow, provided an editing workshop and feedback on grammar, punctuation and style for this anthology. We are extremely grateful for her input.

Cornwall Writers Short Story Project

This anthology has a rich variety of stories – of different genres, time periods and moods. No single story gives any clue to the next.

The stories weave together as contrasts: each enhances and is enhanced by those around it. Beginning with an engaging holiday read set in Cornwall, the collection ends with a place in Cornwall waiting for someone to visit and love it. There are ebbs and flows, surprises and entertainment throughout. And if you enjoy our stories half as much as we did putting them together, you will fall in love with them!

The ideas and words for our theme have many meanings and creative angles. Our aim is to provoke curiosity in whoever picks up the book.

Words can suggest particular genres, so we voted on three favourites that combine into a theme open to a wide interpretation. The theme became the title – *Cornwall: Misfits, Curiosities and Legends.*

The Cornwall Writers Short Story Project is a community of writerly friends committed to honing our writing and editing skills and learning how to publish, market and sell books.

This project began in January 2019 and has taken 18 months to complete. We have had the pleasure of seeing each other's stories develop and grow into the works contained in this book.

Cornwall Writers
Cornwall: Misfits, Curiosities and Legends

Short Stories and Other Scribbles

Wade Beneath The Waves

by Emily Charlotte Ould

It's half-term. It's nearly summer. And I'm at Granny and Granddad's house in Cornwall.

I'm sat in an orange armchair surrounded by orange walls, stroking the orange curtains that feel all soft like the fuzzy peaches Mum makes me eat.

I think Granny likes orange.

Granddad sits beside me – in another orange armchair. He's even eating an orange right this second, with his feet up on the stool watching TV. The smelly orange peel sits on a plate, all curled up like a sneaky snake. Granddad doesn't like snakes.

But Granny definitely likes orange.

I watch Granddad eat the fruit, pulling off each segment, and I laugh as juice dribbles down his chin. He wipes his mouth and grins at me, before popping the rest of it whole into his mouth.

I wonder if he likes oranges, or whether Granny makes

him eat them just because. I think, secretly, Granddad likes cakes and chocolates. Like me.

'Are you ready to go?' Granny shouts from the hallway. 'Have you got your shoes and socks on?'

'Yes!' we shout back.

I thump my trainers against the floor and watch them light up in bright blue, green and yellow. Granddad winks at me, wiggling his slippers about on top of the stool.

'D'you want a chocolate bourbon, Wade?' he asks, switching the TV channel, then slips his hand beneath the armchair. He pulls out a biscuit tin with a teddy bear on the front. The teddy bear looks at me like it's whispering, 'Go on. Have one!'

I dip my hand into the biscuit tin and shovel one into my mouth. I swallow it down quick – before Granny comes in and sees.

'Come on then, you two. Let's not waste the day away!' Granny pads into the living room in her sparkly sandals. Today she's wearing a long floaty dress, big sunglasses and red lipstick, with a floppy white hat sitting elegantly on her head.

'You look pretty, Granny,' I say, jumping up from my chair.

'Thank you, Wade. Now what,' she tuts at Granddad, 'are you doing sitting there with your bloody stinking feet up? Honestly, anyone would think you're the seven-year-old, not Wade. Come on, put your shoes on.'

'Alright, alright,' he grumbles, kicking one slipper off into the air. It lands with a thud on the orange carpet.

Granny passes him his shoes.

'Race you to the car!' I shout.

'Wait, wait!' Granddad says. He's staring at the TV. 'Look 'ere.'

He turns the TV up. On the screen, there's a tall building, as tall as the ones I see all the time back home in London with Mum. But this one is in flames and suddenly there are lots of firefighters on the screen. They're spraying a long hose up at the building, but there are people inside. They can't reach. I look at the floor.

'Poor souls,' Granddad says. 'Never bloody stood a chance.'

'John,' Granny says, then turns the TV off. 'Not in front of Wade.'

'Sorry,' Granddad murmurs, then switches the TV off at the wall. 'Better get going, eh, squirt?' He ruffles my hair.

'Your mum is a very brave lady doing what she does, you know,' Granny says as I bounce towards the door. 'She helps so many people.'

'I know,' I say, even though I'm not really sure what she's talking about. 'Does it have something to do with that building on fire? Is that why she can't stay down here on holiday too?'

'Something like that,' Granny says, and smiles.

As we're walking towards the car, the lady next door called Meirwen steps out of her house. She sees me in my shorts with my bucket and spade and asks where we're going.

'To the beach! To make sandcastles! And splash in the waves!' I shout.

'Oh,' she says in her funny voice that sounds like music, 'isn't that won-der-ful? Here, poppet, have a biscuit.' She goes back inside her house and brings out a biscuit tin. This one is even bigger than Granny and Granddad's biscuit tin, which I think is strange because Meirwen lives all on her own and has nobody to share them with. I decide she must really like biscuits.

'What do you say, Wade?' Granny asks, slipping her book into her handbag.

'Thank you, Meirwen,' I say and smile before jumping in the car.

'C'mon then!' Granddad says, slamming my door shut behind me. 'Enough yapping for one day. Let's go to Whipsiderry beach!

The sand pulls at my toes like syrup, all thick and wet. It's like quicksand; in places, it swirls like it's alive, dribbling water back to its rock pools where all the crabs and fishes live. We had to climb down hundreds of steps to get here. It was like marching down a giant staircase in a castle leading to a dungeon, but instead of darkness we can see as far as forever with bright, blue sky above us and the great big ocean in front.

The waves come in all at once, and then all the way out again, taking it in turns. Right in front of me, foam sprays off the waves like steam from the shower, curling up and up until it disappears into the sky. Little black dots line the waves, moving fast and all in zigzags, and I point and laugh at them until Granny tells me they're surfers – people who like the ocean more than they like the land.

'I bet the buggers would breathe water if they could,' Granddad says.

Watching them float up and down against the waves, I wonder what surfers look like up close. I wonder whether they have gills like fish and whether, when they speak, if they speak in bubbles.

I bet the buggers would if they could.

Once we've had our sandwiches, I tell Granddad to find a bin quick before all our rubbish is swept into the sea and hurts the world. Mum says it's bad to leave rubbish anywhere. I charge around with my pirate's sword in the air, leading Granddad towards the nearest bin so it's not left on the beach.

Then it's time for sandcastles – my favourite part of all. We make a really big one that has a moat and everything. It's just missing one thing. I run to the dark cave on the far side of the sand. On the rocks sit a thousand mussels and I try to scratch them off with my spade to stick on my castle as jewels, but once Granddad catches up with me, he tells me off.

'Those are mussels, Wade. Living things. You don't wanna hurt them, do 'e?'

So I scramble off the rocks and pat the mussels one by one and whisper 'sorry' into their ears – or where I think they have ears – and run back to where Granny is reading a book about different colours of grey.

We finish off our sandcastle with pink shells Granddad helps me find near rockpools. They make even better jewels. I stand back and admire our work.

'What shall we do now, Granddad?' I ask.

'I don't know 'bout you, but I'm knackered, Wade.' Granddad plonks his bum on the warm sand. 'Why don't you play by yourself while I rest a minute?'

'Okay,' I say. 'Can I hunt for crabs?'

'Knock yourself out.'

I run off towards the rockpools on the far side of the beach.

'Just stay in sight!' Granny and Granddad yell behind me.

Soon, I find the biggest rockpool I've ever seen. It's so big it looks like a massive lagoon and the tide is coming up against the rocks, making waves splash over the sides. I can still see Granny and Granddad if I lean around the curve of the cliff. But when I crouch down and bend my face towards the water, all I can see is sea creatures – starfish, hermit crabs, anemones and even small fishes that dart between the rocks. Down here, it's like a whole other world.

I press my hands into the water, run them through the slippery seaweed and smell the salty air. My knees even get wet from the rocks. The waves are coming in fast all around me but I go deeper and deeper into the rockpool.

Then, my feet slip on some seaweed right at the bottom and, before I know it, my head dunks beneath the waves. Everything goes dark. I try and open my eyes, but all I can see is black and it stings. I thrash about but the seaweed is dragging me down. I can't think. I shout out and the ocean fills up my mouth. It tastes like a black pot of salt.

'HELP!' I try to shout, but all that comes out is bubbles.

Then, out of nowhere, a face appears in front of me. It's dark and tangly and wild and it reaches its arms out towards me. I shake my head as fast as I can and try to swim away. What does it want? I want to go home!

Then I feel hands on me – are they hands or are they fins, or even tentacles? – and I can't get away. They grab me and pull me and twist my body away from the water.

My foot gets untangled from the seaweed and I'm pulled out of the water. I can see the sky. I'm gasping for breath. I cough and splutter and urge, but nothing comes out.

'Y'alright there, li'l' snapper?' I hear a voice say.

I look up. This creature is the weirdest one I've ever seen. It stands on two legs, like me, but has dark leathery skin all over its body, apart from its face and its hands. For hair, it has long dark seaweed coming down in waves like the ocean. Its entire body is dripping with water.

And then I know.

This creature must be a merman.

I eye him warily, taking in his long, dark hair and twinkling eyes. He's smiling at me. Slowly, I nod my head and stand up in front of him.

'Gave us a real fright there, didn't you?' he says. Then, when I don't reply, he says, 'Where are your parents, li'l' dude?'

'My mum is in London. She helps people.'

'Okay.'

'Do you live in the sea?' I ask him. If he is a merman, I've got a thousand questions to ask. Like, what's it like to breathe underwater? Does he have any scales? Where's his tail anyway? Does it turn into legs when he saves people on land?

He just laughs. 'Well, practically, yeah. I spend all my life out there on the water, riding the waves.'

I bet he must do that on his seahorse.

'Will you show me? I've always wanted to live in the sea,' I tell him.

'Yeah, anything. What d'you wanna know?' He starts thwacking his great big merman feet against the sand, making dark footprints as he goes. I follow his long, loping great strides. It's hard to keep up with a merman!

'I want to know everything!' I skip along the sand. 'Show me your ways of the sea.'

'Alright, but we're not going too deep. Not after what I've just had to drag you out of. The tide's coming in fast. Don't you know you shouldn't go in the water if you can't swim?'

'I can swim. Actually, I'm best in my class at school!' I poke my tongue out at him. He does it right back.

'Well, alright then.' He laughs, leading me over to another rockpool. 'But you should have some respect for the ocean and all its creatures who live there. It's not a toy.'

'I know that.' I remember Mum's words about looking after our planet.

'That's good, buddy. The ocean is like a whole other world. Did you know that humans only know about 5% of the ocean floor? The rest of it is too deep and dangerous to explore. There could be swimming dinosaurs down there, man, and we wouldn't even know it.'

'Or giant sharks,' I add.

'Exactly! You get it, man.'

We come to a rockpool, a big one far away from the tide, and squat down on our knees. The merman pulls his hair back away from his face so he can see better and stares hard into the pool.

'So, what are we looking for?' I ask, watching him dip his merman fingers quietly into the cool, clear water.

'Devil crab. They're the meanest crabs out there with red, gleaming eyes. I always look for them, but I've never found one.'

'Will you hurt it?' I ask.

'No,' he laughs. 'Think humans have done enough damage to the earth's sea creatures, don't you? I just want to see it. I never hurt any marine life. They've got it hard enough as it is.'

'That's what Mum says,' I tell him proudly.

'Your Mum sounds pretty cool, man.'

When we can't find any devil crabs, the merman stands up. 'C'mon, we'd better get you back. Where are your people?'

'My Granny and Granddad?'

'Yeah. They here?' He looks at me. I stand up too, but not before splashing my hand in the cold rock pool water.

'I'll show you,' I tell him, leading the way off the rock pool edge and down onto the muddy sand.

When we get to Granny and Granddad, their eyes are huge. Granny looks like she's been crying. As soon as they see me, they hug me too tight.

'Where've you been, Wade?' Granny kisses my hair. 'We were about to call the coastguard!'

But I only look at my merman, knowing they'll be amazed to see one in real life. Now we'll have loads to tell Mum!

'He had a little fall in the water,' the merman says. 'But he's alright now.'

'Thank you,' Granny says, still not letting me go. 'Thank you!'

'No problem. You might have a li'l' adventurer on your hands.' He shakes some water from his hair. 'I'd keep your eye on that one.'

'Say goodbye to the nice surfer, Wade,' Granny says,

holding me close.

Surfer? But he's a merman. He's my merman.

'Dylan.' The merman just nods. 'Nice to meet you, Wade. You be careful out on the beach next time. The sea is beautiful, but she can also be dangerous.'

'Thanks, lad,' Granddad says and pats him on the shoulder.

I frown. Have I been talking to a real-life surfer after all? He didn't even speak in bubbles, like I thought. Then, before I can say anything, the merman – Dylan – turns and walks away across the sand. I watch him run towards the sea.

As we make our way back to the car, I turn round to catch a glimpse of my merman one last time.

I don't see him, but wherever he is I know he's going back beneath the waves.

Back where he belongs.

Drowning Horses
by Philip S Rollason

Beats of a modern Jazz solo, somehow finding a scattered rhythm, the edges of blades cutting into the earth. Starting out of sequence, the order somehow switching back on itself, finding its beginning, and, as the thud thud thud chopped about the trees, the three of them cut down through roots and earth, heaping nature's spoils to the side.

They all kept a clean tool, any less and you'd be out to begging, but it was Petherick who had the simple discipline to keep the finest. 'Clean by night,' he'd sing. 'Clean by night and sharpen by morn. The ale and the bread they shall not spoil. Smile then by eve, to bed thy maid, as rust on shovel shall dig thy grave.'

No overhangs. No slopes. The sides must run straight down.

Sweat blurred Petherick's vision, stinging his eyes, a fog over his judgement. He blinked it away, an instinct born of dust-blackened arms and never-to-be-cleaned sleeves and, as the pit coalesced beneath him, he struck down again, cutting in at the corner furthest from the officer. His effort fell a few degrees short of the perfect ninety and so his great back arched, muscles coiled, and as he struck down again the pride of his father took at his core.

Go again now boy. Strong and fine. We're making swiss watches with a trip hammer.

Digging a hole was digging a hole, and a dirty business it could be too, but even under the officer's duress, Petherick would square off the corners just right. Just like his father had taught him. He hid in that ruthless inheritance, in those mantras that had driven him on, that had brought him to this. He was a machine stabbing into the earth, he was discipline, he was exactitude. His movements automated, his action was perfect and with the short side now running straight he notched in at the long edges of the rectangular pit, the smoke from Yorkie's stale cigarettes swaying all about him. It was the first thing the officer had taken. He gestured as if Yorkie had a choice, then he burned up a months-worth of tabs in less than an hour. Yorkie's face curled at the edges but he kept on with his grim work regardless, hiding that hateful longing gaze, knowing it would please the officer more than his old saved up tobacco ever could. The sweet flat smell was caught up in a gust, twisting it over the last of the three grave diggers. Welsh didn't error in his duty. He understood what the officer had them doing, and yet he kept his spade true and his tears honest.

And he dug.

And he cried.

They'd been caught up on the hill, picking slowly through the undergrowth, their boots rolling silently over twigs and leaf litter, spades slung over their shoulders with the self-assured coolness of industry. The officer's unintelligible order had come coupled with a furrowed brow, casting a furtive look in his eyes. Petherick could hear his father in his head joking: *Just your luck boy, not only àve you no idea what he's on about, he àd to have an accent didn'he?* He smiled the beginnings of a giggle. Then the officer swung the rifle from his shoulder and they all three shrunk back at its hollow point.

The woodland floor levelled up to Petherick's chest now, he looked across to Yorkie and Welsh, their graves hardly deep enough to cover the smell, and yet he dug on in that perfectly angled demise, unknowing of what else to do.

The rise and the fall.

The rise and the fall.

The rise... He stalled at the top of his drive. A turning pink half-worm flicked and writhed at its unknown severance, corkscrewing from the flat black wall of his grave, its other half tossed to the heap above. He thought to care that the officer had seen him stop, but a surge of indifference held his spade. He could so easily have felt the bullet burn into him before the crack of the rifle had even registered. He half wished for it. But he never turned to ask. He just stared as the undying half-thing squirmed on. *Shoot me*, he thought. *And if you shoot me now, will I be forever living and un-living as the two halves of this worm?*

Then he felt the tug. A siren's call. The cut end slowing, flashing, rocking like a wrecker's light. Petherick stooped down to touch it, to feel the blind indignant life in this ridiculous thing, and, as his finger kissed against the wound, his flesh and the flesh of the worm swelled at their contact. He felt to pull back and he sensed the thing twitch in retreat. They both paused, as if imagining what this moment could possibly be. Then, with absolute consensus, it ate him and he ate it and the half-worm slipped effortlessly into the end of his finger, his skin sealing around its entry. And like that, it was in him. He pulled his hand up, turning it in the air, flexing his fingers. It was such a strange thing to have happened in such an ordinary way and now that it was in him he couldn't feel it there at all. Perhaps it was tunnelling into his flesh now, digging in his muscles or swimming through his veins? Or perhaps it would burrow its way up to his head, eat his eyes blind and take over his senses in retribution for chopping the worm in two?

Petherick rolled his shoulders. He still felt strong, he still felt useful. He knew what the officer planned to do and yet he still felt good. He rubbed his thumb over the end of the worm-finger, then he looked to the place in his tomb's wall where the worm had been cut in two and something caught his eye. There, in the tiny alcove left by the worm, a nub of gold flashed up at him. He reached down to pull it free. At first his finger twitched against the wall, pushing and testing for the right place. Then, all at once it dug in up to the knuckle, turning and pulling at the earth, tugging and pressing to find its treasure. The prize set to his palm, it was cold and hard. He clawed at it with his worm-possessed hand, pulling the metallic-yellow ore from the wood and leaves of a forest long dead, then he stole it to his pocket feeling that the officer must surely be standing above him, rifle trained down, angry that Petherick had perhaps found his fortune. He steeled himself and looked around only to see the officer asleep against the bough of a tree, the gun in his lap. His heart quickened as he looked to Yorkie and Welsh. The Yorkshireman was still heaving his spade through the motions and, just beyond him, Welsh dug on, two great white streaks through the dirt on his face where the all-but-dried-up tears had tracked down his cheeks.

'Psst.' Petherick hissed to interrupt their cadence. 'Psst!' The two miners hadn't heard him. 'Hey,' he said, glancing back to the officer. 'He's asleep.' Welsh flashed a frightened look to Petherick and then to Yorkie. Then he turned his back and picked up the pace of his rhythm. 'Hey,' he said again, surely they hadn't understood. 'He's asle-'

'No,' said Yorkie, his head a slow stoic shake.

'Look-' began Petherick, but his protest was cut short. It had begun to rain.

A single crack split the forest as the first coin sparked from the side of Petherick's helmet. It ricocheted to crack once more against the stock of the rifle, and there it lay in the officer's lap, all shiny and new and wanting to be had. The officer snapped awake, groping at the rifle, his eyes jumping between the coin and the three of them, scrabbling for what had happened at the end of his dream, fumbling for the line where consciousness took over. Still half in the sleeping and half in the waking he rose to his feet, the coin falling from his lap. He looked down as it curled to a halt, then he looked to Petherick and his face turned to contempt, his instinctive suspicion somehow piecing it all together. He barked out in unknown words yet Petherick understood him completely.

You threw this, he was saying.

He pulled the rifle up and nestled its butt into his shoulder, his stance suddenly cold and professional and trained. Then, in that unreal silence before a bullet is fired, another crack rung out about them. A newly minted coin, manna from heaven, had clipped the edge of the officer's helmet. The rifle slackened as he first looked to the coin on the floor and then up to the leaves above. A slow broad smile slipped across his face and he purred new words that the three of them knew all too well. Then, all at once, ripping through the canopy, money of all currencies and denominations fell from the sky. Shredded leaves fell in zig-zags while newly printed banknotes twirled and danced amongst the death-von-verdant. The officer danced in a circle while the three miners looked on, money spilling into their pits, covering their boots to the ankle. The officer was laughing now, laughing and scooping notes and coins into his pockets, and when his pockets were full and the money bulged at the seams inside his jacket and trousers, he took off his belt and began to stuff more into his underwear. It was a ludicrous sight, the frantic ecstasy at which the officer grabbed and hoarded made him look like a drunk with the keys to the brewery or like a political cartoon, his gaping smile somehow drawn with each tooth the same size. He was forcing fistfuls of notes up his jacket front now so that he looked pregnant with it.

Petherick heard the snapping of Yorkie before he saw him striding past, splashing coins ahead of him and sending banknotes twirling about his boots.

'No,' Yorkie had said again. Then he started at the officer who, in his rapture, had turned his back to them, his arms held up to the sky, laughter convulsing through him. A bucking machine. But just as Yorkie had begun to lift his spade, that intuitive suspicion yanked the officer back to his duty and in an instant he wheeled around swinging the stock of his rifle low and up into Yorkie's stomach. Petherick's hole was so deep now that, when Yorkie hit the floor, their eyes met. They held each other for an instant, a sadness between them, until Petherick could bear to look no more and he shuttered his eyes. But Yorkie's slack face remained hung in the red behind his eyelids.

Then in a flash he was home. He was a boy again, looking down at Yorkie's desperate face bobbing frantically in the cold black water.

The mare had been lost all day. And as the evening mist curtained the night, Petherick had run up to the old quarry. 'She'll have beaten us home by now,' his father had said. 'C'mon now with me and your brother and we'll find her in the master's yard, scared from the lightning.' But when he reached the edge of the flooded pit he could see that he hadn't time to go for help. The old girl was tired, her head hardly breaking the surface, the sides of her nose raw from nudging at the sheer quarry walls. Horror-stricken, Petherick stood and watched to give the horse solace, and, as if in desperate response, the mare's eyes grew wild, tears pooling at the red edges. Then he saw Yorkie's face again, framed in the unending depths of the flooded quarry, desperation in every breath, as if to sink would be to desert Petherick and Welsh at his last. His nostrils flared, sucking in clumps of soil he'd dug from the ground, turning the frothing spit around his nose and mouth a rich soil-black. And as Yorkie spluttered and coughed, a coin stuck in his throat, the old mare slipped down into the cold black abyss with barely a ripple and nary a sound. Petherick opened his eyes just as the officer raised Yorkie's spade, and shame twisted in him as he turned away, catching the despair in Welsh's face as a thud split down into the earth.

When he turned back, Yorkie had been rolled away. The officer stood above him pointing the rifle, shooting down with other-worldly orders to do other-worldly things.

Bury him, the officer was saying.

And so it was that the rhythm started up once more. But now the synchronisation was between just the two. A simple yet off-kilter beat that kept the two rhythms apart, only then for them to find each other. Like two siblings, separated at birth, meeting on an empty street, their passing known only to kismet as they walk on, back-to-back, away from each other.

Finding and losing.

Finding and losing...

Then Welsh broke too. Petherick had heard his strains and knew it was only a matter of time. He lurched forward, anger pushing him at the officer, but in his rage he slipped on the last of the money that had yet to soak away and he knew his chance had passed. The rifle snapped against the officer's shoulder and Welsh too was rolled down into the ground. Then just as before, with cold certainty, the officer ordered Petherick to fill the hole.

And he did.

One chop now. One spade, one beat. Petherick worked alone. The officer lit up the last of Yorkie's cigarettes and watched him toil as Welsh followed Yorkie, one more drudge to sink down into the mare's abyss. Then, when he had smoothed the graves and cried his goodbyes, the officer ordered him down into his own perfect tomb.

It felt like rain. Not the rain of notes and coins but the gentle patter of the churnings of nature, and that sensation surrounded him, and the surrounding pressure consumed him. In ten minutes he was deep within the earth. A minute more and Petherick was asleep.

When he woke, fetal within the rich decay of the earth's renewal, he could hear it was raining again. The soft thud thud thud on the forest floor that would draw up the worms to feed the waiting birds. He could feel that soft wet drumming calling him up, and so Petherick became the worm and the worm became him and he blindly pulsed up through the soil, eating and writhing, old twigs and spent leaves sliding past his squirming smooth body. He pulled himself up to the surface, his nose and mouth breaking through, sucking in at the cool autumn air. Wriggling an arm free, as the rain washed the dirt from his eyes, he pulled himself up and out and stood above his grave, blackened soil staining his clothes and face. Coughing, retching as a pile of mud fell from his mouth, he cleared his nose and pulled clumps of soil from his ears, and that's when he heard it. The officer's laugh echoing through the forest. Petherick spun on the spot, looking for the villain, catching sight of the back of the officer's head as he walked the path down the hill, back to the city. Once more Petherick rolled silently across the forest floor, gaining on the officer with ease. He reached into his pocket and pulled out the shining yellow rock and as he crept to within striking distance he raised his arm to mutiny, the rush of revenge granting warrant to the sin at hand.

Petherick's final beat was on measure, its timing was true and its trueness was sweet. He drove his fist down, a golden flash in the air, but as it hit into the back of the officer's head it made no sound at all. He pitched forward, stumbling off-balance as his blow passed straight through the officer as if he were a phantom. The officer stopped and, without turning, in his other way of speaking, he said, *Pyrite.* Petherick froze. He could hear the smile on the officer's face, he could feel the weight was wrong. He'd known it when the half-worm had guided him to its hiding place and yet he'd taken it all the same. Just in case.

'Fool's gold,' Petherick said, and he looked over its dull shine in his hands. Then he collapsed to the floor as the officer walked away, whistling to the trees as he disappeared down the hill.

Petherick remained, Pyrite cradled in his hands, polishing the worthless lump with the blackened cuff of his sleeve, checking for his reflection before turning it over and buffing it again. And as time passed and the trees gave way to industry, and the industry gave way to policy, people came from the corners of the world unknowingly searching in innocent marvel for Petherick's drowning horses.

Barnacle Bill

by Caroline Palmer

Barnacle Bill was born in Bedruthan Steps and had spent all his life there. He didn't think much of anybody at all, and particularly kept himself to himself where women were concerned: he had just no time for them. Bill's nickname came from the fact that he enjoyed barnacles by the bucket load and would fix the shells onto the walls of his dilapidated-looking white cottage. The cottage was like an expression of Bill's personality – it had thick granite walls and a well thatched roof, but the walls were badly in need of a lick of paint. The cottage was scruffy like Bill, but solid as well.

He had inherited the cottage from his father who had got it from his father; the family had lived in the village for as long as anyone could remember. They were all remembered for their eccentricity, and Bill was no different. His father had been well known for making unkind comments such as 'You take your boat out today and you won't catch anything!' This was inevitably said with an evil leer on his face, so the other fisherman had avoided him when they were going out, as, uncannily, he was often right.

All the villagers were cautious of Bill too as he had a sharp tongue and didn't tolerate fools. He lived on his own with his black and white cat, Magpie, for company and held long, one-sided conversations with her. In Bill's opinion, Magpie made more sense than any darned woman, or man too. She was his soft spot and people would have been surprised to hear him crooning away to her. However, one of the visitors to the village found him totally fascinating.

Winnie from Wisconsin, USA, was visiting her cousin, Jane Hoskin, and was determined to make friends with Bill. Winnie had taken a fancy to him the moment she clapped eyes on him, scrutinising a tray of beef steaks in the local butchers. She was attracted by his aloof air and well-built figure and she liked his scruffiness too. Winnie did her very best to hunt him down and have a conversation with him, but had no luck. When Jane Hoskin discovered what was going on, she commented scornfully 'You don't want to be involved with that miserable old scoundrel! His expression is enough to turn milk sour!!' However, this only made Winnie more determined to get to know Bill; she was sure that he couldn't be that grumpy. He must be misunderstood instead!

Bill was completely unused to all this attention from a woman and had to work out a way to avoid her persistent approaches as, with crafty foresight, she guessed where he might be and went there to meet him. He gave up staying home in the daytime after Winnie banged on his door a dozen times and then walked in without being invited. She gave him a big smile and said, 'I'd like us to be friends!' and sat down in his favourite chair. Bill's instinct was to run for it, out of the front door. So he did that, shouting, 'I don't want no friends, thanks very much!' Bill resented her behaviour; he was having his work cut out to avoid her.

The infatuated Winnie texted her friends back in the USA. 'You should meet my Cornish curiosity! Here's a photo I took when he wasn't looking! I'm not giving up on him. See you sometime in October!' Winnie's friends wondered who it was this time, but then they were used to her ways. She would take a passionate liking to a man for a few months, and then drop him, and then find another one to rant on about. Currently Winnie seemed to be obsessed with Bill and determined to catch up with him, however well he tried to hide.

Bill tried going into the Village Social Club, the Men Only section, even though he wouldn't normally cross the threshold, but when he left there, Winnie would be waiting outside. He walked on the cliffs for hours, only to find her coming the other way. Forced into desperate measures, he found himself climbing a tree to escape Winnie's approaching form; it worked, but he could hardly stay up a tree all his life. He was up there for hours, to be on the safe side, before he stiffly slid to the ground, looking warily both ways as he did so. Eventually he decided to take his boat out every day that he could; at the furthest end of the harbour felt the safest place to be. Surely Winnie could not track him down out there! For the first day, all was calm and peaceful; Bill took a succulent pasty and a bottle of beer with him. He and the boat rocked in unison in the place just before the harbour joined the sea. The water was calm and the harbour not overfull of boats.

Bill enjoyed having a snooze in the sun and relished the feeling of peace and quiet. He relaxed deeply and, enjoying swigs of his favourite beer, he munched on his pasty with contentment in his heart. Peace and quiet at last! He would have to pick some barnacles soon to keep him going, but a day or two off wouldn't hurt. It felt as though the old uneventful days had returned. When he would feel safe to return to his house in daylight, Bill didn't know, but 'I'll just make the most of this restful day!' he thought.

Bill stayed in the harbour till the evening, then he moored the boat and cautiously made his way home to the cosy cottage and miaowing Magpie. Bill drew the curtains after taking a discreet look around outside and was delighted to see no sign of Winnie. He cooked himself eggs and bacon; it was nice and easy and he didn't feel like doing much that evening, then he opened another bottle of beer and put on the TV, feeling that all was well with his world. The football was on, and he was soon lost in the game. Bill nodded off in the chair, going up to bed a bit later, muzzy headed but content.

The next day dawned fine and sunny, and after making some ham sandwiches and taking a bottle of cider, Bill headed for the harbour, keeping a weather eye out for Winnie. There was no sign at all of her buxom form nor echo of her loud American voice. He breathed a sigh of relief. Bill closed his eyes and prepared to nod off; he was still needing to catch up after the difficult couple of weeks he'd had. He was very satisfied at how things were going.

'It's got better!' he thought, reflecting with relief that he could do what he wanted to for now, and sooner or later, if he toughed it out, Winnie would have to return to to Wisconsin. However, if he had read the text she had sent her friends some time ago, he might have worried more! Bill's eyes briefly opened and he scrutinised the harbour carefully. There was no sign of anything disturbing, so he shut his eyes again and slept.

He was woken suddenly by the boat rocking violently and a well-known American voice yelling in his ear. 'You sure are hard to find but I tracked you down!' Standing up in her canoe, Winnie's hands were grasping the side of the boat as she prepared to board. Bill was furious and pushed her hands off, leaving Winnie wobbling in her canoe. Suddenly the canoe overturned and she fell into the water. Frantically yelling for his help, Winnie clung to the side of the canoe and then let go, attempting to swim for the shore. Bill looked at her feeble efforts and an unusual feeling of sympathy came over him.

He shouted 'Keep swimming, girl. I'm coming!'

He rowed the boat towards her, but it was clear he wouldn't get there in time, so he dived in and swam towards Winnie's almost submerged body. He dragged her behind him and after a short time they reached the edge of the harbour.

A small crowd of onlookers had gathered, fascinated by the unlikely sight of Bill dragging Winnie through the water. Bill ignored them entirely and concentrated on her.

'Have you got any dry clothes anywhere?'

'No, nothing except at my cousin's.'

'Well, we'll have to go up there, won't we?'

And to the onlookers, he yelled 'You lot there! Stop smirking! Haven't you got any homes to go to?' They all looked embarrassed, but after Bill and Winnie had left, guffaws broke out anew.

The villagers grew used to the new order of things after a time. Where Bill was, Winnie was too. Every day they could be seen out together, chatting away. And Winnie even learned to like barnacles. She also sent a text to her American friends saying 'I'm a Cornish curiosity now. Expect me when you see me!' But they never did! While Bill might have taught Winnie to like barnacles, she taught him how to smile.

Waiting

by Anita D Hunt

*P*enzance, *April 1758*

It was dark when he left. It would be hours until the sun rose to herald the start of a new day. Alice was used to it, of course. Yesterday she'd begged him not to go, to stay with her and the children.

'Tis easy money, maid,' he'd replied in that chiding Cornish lilt of his. 'Can't make anywhere near as much in a month on the farm as I can do in one night out there.' He pointed in the direction of the cliffs.

'But the tide? What if—'

'Dun' 'e fear 'bout no sea, I knaw's what she be 'bout. She'll never hurt me lass.'

'I can't help but be afraid.'

He had grabbed her shoulders and planted a kiss on her forehead. 'I'll bring us back a nice keg o' brandy. That'll take your fears away.'

He'd kissed her on the forehead again this morning, gently whispered 'goodbye' before slipping out of the bedroom, closing the door quietly behind him. She didn't say goodbye or even acknowledge his leaving. She didn't want him to think he had her blessing. She could never give him that. She heard the front door close and opened her eyes, peering around in the dark, hoping he would walk back in again. She would not go back to sleep now, not until he returned. She told herself she was being ridiculous; he'd done this a hundred times and he always came back.

As the moon went lower, she stoked the fire back into life and put the kettle on the stove to warm the water for his tea. As the sun began to rise, she prepared his breakfast of bread and dripping. He'd be hungry when he got back. It was such hard, physical work he had to do. She refilled the boiled-dry kettle and put two thick slices out for him, they could spare it with what he was going to bring in from the boat. The children stumbled in, bleary eyed and tousle-haired, eager to tuck into the feast on the table. She tapped the backs of their outstretched hands with the ladle.

'That's Pa's for when 'e gets back,' she told them. 'Keep your thievin' mitts off and go get your own.'

'Where's 'e gone Ma?' Mary asked, clambering onto her chair and staring longingly at the forbidden meal on the table.

'Just out, he'll be back soon. Edward, get your sister some bread please.'

'She can get 'er own Ma! Why do I always 'ave to get 'er stuff?'

Alice drew in her breath and held it, she didn't want to have any arguments this morning, her nerves were fraught enough already.

'Because she's littler than you an' because I said so.'

Ruffling Mary's hair fondly before turning on her heel, she went to the front door and stood, looking over the moor to where it dipped at the cliff edge and she could see the cold grey blue of the sea beyond.

She closed the door against the icy breeze that blew through the room and started to pace the floor. Ten steps from the fireplace and back again to the kitchen, turn and repeat, give the fire a stoke, turn and repeat. Hands wringing unconsciously as the sun rose higher, approaching the midday hour. Mary and Edward bickering about whose turn it was to feed the chickens, who had to muck out the stable. Alice snapped.

'Edward! Go an' do the 'orses, Mary, the chickens and get the eggs, and dun' 'e drop any mind, we need them for us tea tonight.'

'But I always do the 'orses Ma, tisn't fair!'

'Mary ain't big enough an' you know it, now git out of 'ere before I get teasy good an' proper.'

The children scampered out of the house. In the silence that followed, time dragged even slower. She knew she had been too hard on them, her guilt weighed her down and she stamped her foot in anger at herself. She'd make up for it later, when he came home they'd have a big supper and sing the children's favourite songs to celebrate his booty.

It was far too dangerous for him to still be at the beach at this hour. The night was his cover and the incoming tide his mistress, bidding him to empty the boats while she was closest to the jagged rocks and hidden caves. She would nigh on be at her lowest ebb now, no threat nor help to anyone standing on the shoreline. The mud-caked floors mocked Alice's steps. The cold stone walls suffocated her, claustrophobia forcing her into the yard where she gulped at the brisk, fresh air.

Pulling her shawl tighter around her shoulders, long woollen skirts billowing in the wind that whipped around her, she found herself walking along the path he would have taken this morning, calling to the children to go and see Hilda if they needed anything. She wouldn't be long.

She had to make sure he didn't see her; he'd be so angry if he did. If he knew that she was out looking for him when he'd said he would be back. He was probably just putting the boat away. She'd just glance over the cliff edge, see if he was still there.

The beach was deserted. All that was left were the drag marks of a boat being brought to shore and then pushed out again. This evening's high tide would get rid of them again. Remove the traces of the smuggling that had happened last night.

Maybe it was a different boat? Nothing to do with the bounty. Alice made her way slowly down the cliff path, stepped onto the cold shifting sand as the first drops of rain began to fall. The wind was greater here, whipping around the secluded West Cornwall cove, seeking to find its escape. The waves lashed against the shore. She could see his mistress was angry, attempting to get revenge for the deeds that have happened here. Fear clung even closer to Alice's heart.

She swept her wet hair from her eyes and pulled her shawl tighter around her shoulders before making her way around the perimeter of the beach. She would be able to get into the cave easily now, could see if the delivery had been brought in. She ducked her head and felt the sea-worn smoothness of the rocks under her hands as she slipped through the crevice opening, barely big enough to fit the barrels of brandy through but widening once inside into a hollow area where smugglers from times gone by had fashioned shelves out of the rock to store the barrels above the tide line. A fissure in the roof let in just enough light to see the neatly stacked kegs upon them, a fully stocked larder where last week it had lain empty. He wasn't here, but he had been. He had seen his night's work through.

Making her way back to the beach, her mind was in turmoil. He had to be near. He knew she would be worried. The waves licked back and forth, white foam crashing on the wet sand, reaching out for her and then falling back, regaining its strength and then coming for her again and again. As if hypnotized, she made her way to the sea's edge, walked along it, not caring for her shoes getting wet, her heavy skirts greedily soaking up the water and getting heavier with every step.

She kept walking, following the curve of the water as it ebbed and flowed until she came to the rocky crevice at the end of the cove. A flash of black caught her eye, bobbing in the centre of the largest pool. She reached out to grab it, pulled it to her and, recognising it, clutched it to her chest.

He said it was his lucky scarf. The plain black piece of cotton that he used to tie around his mouth and nose so the guards wouldn't be able to see the white of his face.

'You need to be careful goin' out lookin' like that,' she would say. 'They guards'll think you're out to rob they rich folk.'

'There's worse things t'be hung for than bein' an 'ighwayman, but they'd 'ave to catch me first and I'm too clever for 'em. I knaws where to hide if I see 'em coming and this beauty'll make sure I stay hid. Don't 'e worry lass, I'll be alright.'

She'd purse her lips and decline to answer any more. It wasn't an argument she was ever going to win; he would give her rigid body a hug until she relaxed her head onto his shoulder.

'I'll always come 'ome to you and the cheel's. T'aint no-one as can keep me away.'

The planks battered against the rocks; a broken oar nudged at her feet. Searching amongst the wreckage she found what she didn't want to see. The Mary-Alice name plate glinted at her as the weak, spring sun struggled to break through the dark laden clouds.

She fell to her knees in the ebbing surf. Lifting her head, to stare at the far horizon, she screamed into the void, the wind whipping the sound from her mouth before she could give it a voice. The sea had won their battle for his love and snatched Alice's away, the wind its colleague in keeping the victor's secret.

The mistress had finally become the wife.

Alice would forever be the silent widow.

The Dance of the Stones

by David Allkins

I woke up in my goblin body on a grey Thursday. I switched to the human shape I use for walking about outside, because the extra foot in height is easier for reaching the cupboards. Some fairies have all these glamours to bewitch humans. I'll stick with what's near to me, short fat girl with a buzz cut. I flicked a T-shirt, pants and dressing gown on for trudging down to breakfast.

Over the sugary cereal and coffee, I read about the latest bad omens on the Cornwall fairy network phone app. Increased 'End is Nigh' graffiti, crows feeding on seagulls. Whatever, you've still got to go to work.

When I was officially a knocker goblin, it used to be easy. I'd crawl within the depths of the earth. Then I'd just listen with my fairy hearing for the different sounds of the rocks and use my vibration and drumming powers to lead miners to rich seams. Couldn't let them see me though.

My eyes, ears and head would have looked too big for my frame. The bald head, sharp teeth and greenish-grey luminescent skin wouldn't have helped. A miner panics and there's an accident. I'm fit for a goblin, but humans have no taste.

Then the mining ended and you have to do something else. I pull on the gloves I wear to hide the backs of my hands. Whether human or goblin, they are marked with rocks and gems embedded in them. Then off to Truro, to try and find somewhere to park my green Volkswagen Beetle.

Working at a gem and fossil shop does mean putting up with customers, but it means you can lead them to something they'd want or catches their eye, through low key tapping on display cases and shelves.

It was alright, till I went to buy a lunch of chicken korma pasty and two vegan sausage rolls and was visited by an owl crone. She was at least in no-humans-can-see-me mode.

An owl crone is what it says on the tin, half owl, half old woman. A mass of feathers, saggy faded clothing, hair and wings with massive eyes and a mouth in her beak. Smells like stained cardigans left in an attic. A whole coven of them run the fairy-folk operations of Cornwall. It's like the head of the company coming down to your branch. They call themselves a parliament, but are less forgiving of mistakes.

'Derwa, little knocker maiden.' I put my lunch down and bowed. I'd have curtsied but you can't do that in jeans. She spoke with authority and the sense she might go for your throat.

'We are currently suffering from a theft from our archives by the Catastrophe Junkies, as I believe is the common signifier for them.' Their name used to be something old, long and Latin, but now they are the Catastrophe Junkies. A bunch of mostly human-looking things able to experience amazing psychic highs off disasters and the coverage of them. All fear and despair and loss nourishes them. Basic moral and spiritual vermin. Like vultures without the beauty or nobility.

'What did they take?'

'A large stone, once a human who played one of the forbidden melodies. Given the passions of the Catastrophe Junkies, we doubt this is anything good.' There is always a moment when you realise you've been dragged into the clean-up of a mess.

'As a knocker, Derwa, you have an affinity with rocks and stones. We cannot afford to overlook any possible signs or information. Give me your phone.'

I passed it to her and the fingers danced over the buttons. 'Our contact is now within.'

Her left hand pressed a pea sized fragment into mine, the fingernails pushing into my palm. 'This is one of the remnants of the missing main piece, to study. Any information or omens you find, let us know.'

She leapt up and in a flap of wings was gone. I slowly chewed at my lunch and returned to work.

The evening was spent dragging over my library and human and fairy websites instead of a fun slump in front of the TV. There's lots of stories about dancers or people turned to stone for no good reason. In terms of forbidden magic music, a lot of it is 'play this and something horrible will happen', then someone does it anyway. The nearest I could find to anything near me in Cornwall, was a story about some maidens who went out on one dark and misty Sunday morning to dance on the cliffs and never came back. This story didn't even have any physical stones anywhere to back it up.

I dragged myself to work on Friday, but I realised there was something else I could try. When I got home, I had a quick, light snack. Then I turned down all the lights, drew the curtains and put the cloth with the magic markings over the carpet. I got down to my underwear, changed back to my goblin state, picked up the small piece of stone the owl crone had given me and lay on the floor. My left hand locked around it.

Focusing into the right state of mind is like meditation. You're tuning yourself to the information within the stone, to see what it's recorded. Every stone has a history, knocker goblins are the ones who can read them.

I was on the Newquay cliffs on a dark and misty morning, feeling the dampness against my skin, hearing the brushing of the waves against the rocks. A circle of young women in long white dresses were dancing in a strange wild twisting style. In the middle, there was a young man in a smart hat and jacket over his ragged clothing. The instrument he was playing was like a mandolin with dead and twisted things fused to it. The sound of the strings was higher and deeper than was possible. The player was singing in a language I couldn't make out, but which didn't sound good whatever it was. His voice was loud, deep and confident.

The skies echoed with thunder, the rain grew in

thickness and power. It beat down on the dancers causing them to slip on the grass, making green marks on the white skirts. The thunder rose to drown out the words of the song. The dancers and musician froze, turned grey, indistinct and expanded. All of them had turned to stone. The stone which had been the music player, stayed on the cliff, rain splashing off it. The other stones around it, slowly sank into the earth, the soil swallowing them like they were sinking beneath water to vanish from sight.

I jolted out of the trance like I was falling in a dream. That part of the Newquay cliffs, I'd walked up and down before, listening to the stories of the stones there. It wasn't even far from where I lived. I could use the fragment like a metal detector to send signals for the rest of the stones if they were down there. Then I'd call the parliament of owl crones, get a pat on the head and they'd know what to do.

I changed back into my human shape, pulled on clothes, added a waterproof jacket and headed off. In a 20 minute walk, I'd made it to the cliffs. I'm only running if a bomb is about to go off. Usually there would be a few people walking dogs but the way to the cliffs was deserted. This should have been a warning to me.

Heading to the area, I saw they'd arrived. A group of male Catastrophe Junkies. All pale, sweaty, too thin or too fat, with clothing which only just fitted or hung on them. They stank of dried-in and fresh sweat. Their deep grey eyes showed up against pale skin. The five of them had a metal cart they were pushing the stone around on. Each of them was holding the stone or cart with a hand to keep it moving. They were heading for a wide area of the cliff. The stone's surface was detailed with cracks and chippings. I ducked down behind one of those metal and wood benches for walkers, mounted on stone slabs, hoping the Junkies didn't notice. As I watched them, I texted the owl crones, hoping the wind could cover any sounds of movement as my gloves creaked pushing buttons.

The Catastrophe Junkies lifted the stone on the ground and crept back. The metal cart was pushed away to roll and fall on its side. They were too busy staring at the stone to look in my direction.

Around the stone, the ones which had been the dancers from my vision, rose out of the earth. No rupturing or scattered earth from them. They just popped out like plastic bottles full of air in water. The greyness of the stone faded away and the dancers were human again. The musician returned as well, although over his form were holes and cracks showing the air and earth behind him. These must have been the parts of the stone lost over the years. The fact of the clean gaps in him, like holes in paper, didn't appear to register. The dancers didn't move or speak, just stood in their white dresses. I saw the Junkies shuffle and shift as if something was going to rush towards them.

The music started playing. The dancing started. I looked up into the clouds which were growing and becoming darker. I could feel the pressure building in the air. The waves were growing bigger and fiercer around the cliff, spraying against the rocks.

Some of the notes in the music seemed familiar. I felt colder when I realised what this spell was. As a goblin, the foreboding feeling was creeping into me. It was a storm-bringing spell. Not just any storm, something more powerful than a hurricane was going to come from nowhere and hit everyone on the coast. Buildings and houses demolished. People trapped and dying in the ruins or pushed over by the wind. Torrential rain stopping the efforts to aid them. All the damage, the loss of life, and the greater it was, the more these little psychic parasites were going to be in bliss from it. Never mind all the people who had died.

Right now, I was the only one who could stop this before it was too late, but in my rising panic I couldn't see how. I started gripping my hands on the stone supporting the bench, then I realised the way to do it.

I pulled off my gloves. The gems and rocks in my flesh were glowing with energy building up for what I had to do. Then I started knocking my knuckles against the stone in a fast series of beats, like a drum solo. If the sound of thunder had got in the way the first time, maybe this could delay the spell.

The sound cut through the chords being played like a drummer doing a different song to the guitarist. Now the high and deep chords of the instrument, were against the hard quick beats of the stone. The Catastrophe Junkies turned and realised I was there. But the knocking sound was cutting into the music, breaking up the force of the spell. I began to speed up the pace as fast as I could, increasing the sound and the rhythm. The dancers started to stumble at the distraction. The musician saw me and his fingers paused, one last note ringing out. For two beats, there was just the sound of me striking the stone, now starting to crack under my hands.

All of them were still, the Junkies, the musician, the dancers. I felt something in the air shift. The dancers and musicians became distorted. Then there was just a stone surrounded by a ring of stones on a cliff edge. They slipped back inside the earth. The clouds parted. The sea became calm, the smack of the waves fading. The wind drained away.

As I used the bench to help pull myself up, the Catastrophe Junkies advanced towards me, fists clenched and snarling, fumbling in pockets for weapons. I wasn't sure if I was going to be able to run or fight, then I heard one of them cry and point up. The owl crones were swooping down, a mass of feathers, clothing and claws. The Catastrophe Junkies turned and bolted from the cliff, not wanting a fight. The crones twisted and swerved in the air to go after them.

One of them turned to land on top of the bench looking down on me. 'We felt a storm of devastation approaching. Well, Miss Derwa, you appear to have prevented a disastrous event and justified our faith in you.'

I tried to smile. 'Thank you.'

'Was the missing stone destroyed?'

I looked at the still grass and earth where all the stones had been. 'I think it's finally back where it belongs.'

Ms Fitt's Lament

by Angela Fitt

What am I doing in Cornwall?
What am I doing down here?
I'm ten years older
than when I arrived,
and I've only been here for a year.

What am I doing in Cornwall?
What on earth am I doing down here?
I'm slow and I'm dreary,
and teary and weary,
and two hours' drive from Ikea.

The man in my life simply loves it.
No commuting; he's free as the air.
He hated the city.
It's just such a pity

I've left all the family there.

The grandchildren...

The man in my life has his boat here.
He has friends and he's feeling relaxed.
He's down at the club,
'Just a small rum and shrub,'
but his partner in life has collapsed.

The life in my man is amazing.
After decades of pressure and strife
he's getting a tan,
and feels like a new man.
So perhaps he just needs a new wife.

It's great that my man is now human.
No frustration, no headaches or grumps;
he's helpful and kind.
So why should I mind?
It's my turn to feel down in the dumps.

I say how I feel, and he listens.
He's upset that I've wilted and shrunk.
He's worried, and feels
like a bit of a heel
sailing gaily ahead, when I've sunk.

'You need a fresh start. A new hobby.'

He wants to be helpful, I think.
'Let's tour the folk clubs
and open-mic pubs.
Find your voice, and your blues will turn pink.

'Or try the gig-rowers, the rare-plant growers,
the silver-band blowers, the spring-seed sowers,
the National Trust goers, the pottery throwers.
And that's just the "O'ers".

'Start at the top with the "A'ers" and "B'ers"
or look through the websites for "Drop in and see
us."
The divers, the bikers,
the drivers, the hikers,
the scribblers, the rhymers,
the fiddlers, the climbers,
horse riders and drummers,
paragliders and mummers.
Or learn a new language, or build a stone wall.
There's really no problem, in Cornwall, at all.'

No... No problem, really, in Cornwall.
Outsiders are welcome whatever.
The misfit can fit in,
the paddler can dip in,
but not when it's
all
too
much

effort.

Oh, really? It's that time already?
I'm sorry for dumping this load.
Just give me a second?
A tissue? I reckon
I'm right at the end of my road.

But thank you for hearing my story,
for sitting there, letting me cry.
I'm drowning. It's bleak,
but I'll come back next week
I promise. I don't want to die.

Flecks of Gold

by Stephen Baird

'Kitto!'

Kitto looked up at the sound of her voice saying his name. His heart lurched. She stood just a few yards away. Beautiful Ysella. And she had just called his name. He put down the pitchfork and blinked, colour rising.

'I can't wait all day,' she called. 'Come here, Kitto.' She beckoned and Kitto found himself moving forward.

She smiled at him and the blood thundered around his heart.

'That's right. Come to me, Kitto. Come on, Kitto. Kitto, Kitto, Kitto.'

He blinked again. Something wasn't right. He wanted it to be, but it wasn't.

'Kitty Kitto,' she coaxed. 'Pretty Kitty Kitto. Come on. Come to Ysella.'

He heard laughter coming from around the side of

the barn and he froze, confused.

Jammes and Jowan, the twins, sprang forward from their hiding place, each linking an arm with Ysella. They turned their backs on Kitto and walked away, laughing. He noticed Jowan slide an arm around Ysella's waist. She laughed louder. Kitto wished it were his arm.

He sighed and sat down on the upturned log that kept the barn door open. He wished he could be more outgoing, could think of clever things to say when they were needed, rather than thinking of them afterwards. He wished he were stronger and taller. The twins were tall for seventeen and Arthek, the blacksmith's son, younger than Kitto, had rippling muscles at sixteen and drew admiring glances from passing girls as he hammered and sweated without his shirt. Then there was Talan, with his black eyes all a-glitter, and his jet hair, always looking at Ysella in a way that made Kitto shudder. As though he was eyeing up a prize animal. And Ysella fanned the sparks of desire.

People rarely noticed Kitto. He was pale, translucent like a spirit and almost invisible. Older women in the village would ask him if he was well when he felt particularly fine.

'Get up, boy!' Kitto leapt up at the command. 'I don't pay you to be idle.'

Kitto looked down. 'I know. I'm sorry Master Trevik.'

'Well get back to work or I'll find somebody with proper muscles who doesn't need to rest.'

The mere hint of dismissal shocked Kitto. Without the farm work, he and his nan would have no money to live by. They had little enough as it was.

'I'm sorry, Master Trevik. It won't happen again.' Kitto followed his employer into the barn.

'Aye,' said Master Trevik more softly. 'Make sure it doesn't.'

The sun was sinking as Kitto headed for home. He stopped, as he always did, and drank in the view, wallowing in the vastness of the moor and intoxicated by the wildness. He had to go there now and run and yell and laugh and become part of the open space. His nan wouldn't mind. She would understand. He reckoned there was still an hour and a half's daylight left. Perfect.

He sat cross-legged on the flat granite, atop the impossibly balanced stack of huge stones. Showery Tor. Smaller than Rough Tor and Brown Willy. Not so high, but this was where he chose to be time and again. He felt at home here. He felt safe here but not everyone thought like that. Many people thought the moor a hostile, dangerous place. That's because they didn't try to understand it. He could think here. Showery Tor was less cluttered, with fewer stones littered round the base of the granite stacks. This was his favourite spot in the world. He had seen little beyond his village that clung to the edge of the moor, but this was a different world.

The sunset had already started. The first streaks of pale gold were painting across the sky just above the horizon. Soon God would have more of his palette on display. Kitto couldn't wait. Full of heart-leaping anticipation. As usual. As always.

Far below, Kitto saw a figure, in the direction of the village. He stared, fascinated. He rarely saw anybody on his visits. He screwed his eyes. Yes, it was Delen the deaf girl. He hardly knew her, though they were almost the same age and had both grown up in the village. She kept stooping and he realized she was picking leaves and flowers for her healing potions and remedies. He pondered for a moment. She didn't fit in easily and nor did he. People mumbled words like 'witch' when she was around, but many were thankful for her healing skills. She could hear nothing and people ignored her because of it. He tried to picture Delen's face, but all he saw was Ysella's.

He turned back to the sunset as streaks of scarlet slashed gently under the vivid turquoise above. Never the same. So, so different each time. Always breath-taking. God the artist creating sunsets for Kitto on Showery Tor. Kitto smiled. His nan wouldn't give God the credit though. She would give it all to Woden.

'I'm home,' he called as he entered the cottage. The smell of stew played at his nostrils. The cottage had just three rooms on one floor. A living space, mainly a kitchen with an antiquated stove, a table and two chairs, and two tiny bedrooms with hard truckle beds and straw-filled mattresses.

'You been on the moor again?' called his nan as she always did.

'Yes,' as he always replied.

The cottage fell silent for a while.

Later, they ate the thin stew together. His nan was always cold so they had a small fire lit.

'Is Woden just a folk tale, Nan?'

'You wouldn't be asking me that, boy, if you had seen the Wild Hunt.'

'Have you seen it, Nan?'

'Aye. And the Lord Woden leading it. He could have taken me as his lover and I would have whooped for the sheer joy of it.'

Kitto looked away, embarrassed. He had never heard Nan talk like this.

'Don't be so prudish, boy! Your old nan has seen things others only have nightmares about. I'm old now but I wasn't once. And if Woden had taken me to be his, I would have not given a backward glance.'

Kitto wasn't sure whether this was just the rambling of old age or desires of the past on one more gallop through fading memories.

'What's he like, Nan?'

'He is the best and the worst, beauty and terror rolled into one. I know, I know. You think I'm rambling in riddles but I remember everything about him.'

She paused, slurping another spoonful of stew noisily, and Kitto screwed his face slightly as droplets ran down her chin through the stubble.

'He is huge and his chariot would dwarf the biggest haycart you've seen. The chariot never touches the ground and nor do his hounds, the wisht hounds of Woden. Their eyes burn red like coals and their slavering jaws could tear you apart in an instant.'

Kitto felt a small quiver work down his spine and he wondered if he should have started this conversation.

'And Woden stands firm and he roars on the wind and laughs to the stars and shakes his great fist at the moon. And if he sees you he will fix his one great golden eye on you and you will quake, before his hounds dispatch you from this world to theirs.'

'Oh,' was all Kitto could say.

He cleared away the supper and washed the bowls outside in the pail of water he had brought back with him from the village pump. Nan started from dozing when he returned.

'Nan?'

'Aye.'

'You saw Woden and survived?'

She nodded, her eyes catching the light of the fire.

'I'm here now, aren't I?'

He nodded. 'So why didn't Woden have you dispatched?'

She cackled with dry laughter. 'Because I knew what to say to stay alive. My ma taught it to me, and her pa before that.'

'Would you teach me?'

'Do you believe in him now?' She leant forward and studied him.

'I – I don't know.'

She nodded. 'Well you had better have worked it out before you meet him.'

'You make it sound like I will meet him.'

'You're a moor lad through and through. You'll meet him one day sure enough. Now listen up and never forget what I'm telling you. If you want to live, that is.'

Kitto listened intently with a mixture of fear and excitement. Fear because it was the difference between life and death, and excitement because Woden sounded like the very life-blood of his beloved moorland, the heart of all wildness. That's how Kitto felt sometimes. So unlike how the villagers saw him, but they didn't understand and never would. Yet every accident on the moor was easily blamed on Woden and his Wild Hunt, and most avoided the moor rather than be drawn to it.

He dragged himself back from his thoughts. Nan was speaking again.

'And don't forget, Woden will give and take away in an instant. He gives gifts like no other, but he will take his payment.'

'But I have no money, Nan.'

She cackled again, a harsh laugh with little humour in it. 'He don't expect money, boy. He'll take what he wants as payment but leave you with something extraordinary and precious.'

Silence. Kitto hung his head and bit his lip.

'Go on, Kitto. You want to ask it but I think you already know.' She stared at him, waiting.

His voice sounded feeble to him. 'What did Woden take as payment from you?'

Nan sighed and said nothing. Kitto thought she might be asleep again. 'Your mother,' she said finally.

Kitto felt his eyes dampening. He knew his mother had died giving birth to him.

'And, what did Woden give to you as a gift?'

'Woden gave me something that was worth the terrible cost.' She paused. 'You were his gift.'

Kitto was very still. It seemed that Woden's payment and gift were both settled the night of his birth. Could that be? He didn't know what to say.

'I shall doze here a while longer, Kitto. You get yourself off to bed. Just remember what I've taught you. And remember, Woden always leaves his mark on those who serve him so everyone knows who belongs to him.'

Kitto saw the firelight catching in her eyes again and only realized, as he slipped into his nightshirt a little later, that the fire had long gone out. He shivered though the night was still warm.

The villagers lined their narrow street as the sky wept unexpected tears over the sombre party making its way along. The pony pulled a low cart on which lay the unmistakable shape of the dead man, under a grubby grey sheet that might once have been white. Behind it walked Father Benesek, the village priest, head down.

Madern the shepherd it was. He went on the moor after a lost sheep late at night and his wife had raised the alarm as light began to break. His body had been found in a treacherous boggy area not far from the village. He had several broken bones, so they said. Three young boys had lost a father, with the wife expecting another child.

Along the street, people crossed themselves as Madern's body passed them. Kitto did the same.

His nan, standing beside him, slapped at his arm. 'Nay, boy, be mindful of antagonizing Woden. This crossing yourself is not for Madern – everyone wants protection from the one responsible for his death. But then they'll tell you they don't believe in Woden.'

Kitto shivered and glanced around nervously, as though Woden might be standing at his shoulder. He wasn't, but Ysella was. Close by. Listening.

The following Sunday, Kitto glanced across the churchyard. The villagers were milling and greeting. He saw Ysella talking to a couple of the village lads. Arthek stood a slight distance away, scowling darkly in his best Sunday clothes. Perhaps Ysella only liked him with his shirt off and the sheen of the forge's heat on him. Kitto scanned around again. The two boys had wandered away and Arthek had disappeared too. Ysella was smiling as she walked towards him.

'Good morning, Ysella,' said Father Benesek approaching them in the dappled morning sunshine, his broad-brimmed hat keeping the brightness at bay.

'Good morning, Father,' said Ysella, lowering her eyelids and flouncing a shallow curtsey. It was all done respectfully and primly but Kitto knew Ysella was intending to look her most alluring. And Father Benesek knew it. The minister turned his gaze away, just before it might have become improper.

'Good day to you, Kitto.'

'Good day, Father.'

'Is your grandmother unwell?' Father Benesek had noticed her usual absence.

'No, Father.'

Silence hung for a moment.

'Kitto's nan prefers other company to God's and yours, Father.' Ysella's voice broke the silence but her words shattered it.

'I'm not sure I know what you mean.'

Kitto looked at Ysella, willing her to drop this. Let it lie like a hare in the field. But he knew she would not.

'Kitto tells me his nan is a follower of Woden.'

The silence returned, frosty in the growing heat of a beautiful summer's day.

Ysella dropped her eyes again, shy and demure.

Father Benesek's face had flushed deeply and Kitto could see beads of sweat glistening under the hat's brim.

Father Benesek looked from Ysella to Kitto. His eyes bored deep into Kitto's. Kitto wanted to stare back innocently but he looked away.

Father Benesek made a strange choking noise, crossed himself and moved quickly away.

'Did I say something wrong?' whispered Ysella. Her smile betrayed her. Kitto wanted to be away. The moor was waiting for him. Calling him.

'I would like to go for a walk with you, Kitto.'

'With me?'

'That's what I said.' Ysella smiled at him again. Run, said his mind, run free. Stay exactly where you are said his heart. This is what you want. Kitto was rooted like an old oak.

'When?'

'This evening.'

He nodded. 'Where?'

'The moor.'

The answer took Kitto's breath away. His mind didn't want her on the moor in case she spoiled it. His heart, however, leapt for joy.

'We could go sooner?'

She shook her head and Kitto could see Arthek returned and waiting impatiently, glowering. 'I have things to do.'

Kitto's head dropped ever so slightly.

There was a touch. Ysella's hand was on his hand. It was cool. Almost icy. 'I won't let you down, Kitto. Just let me know where I can meet you. I'm quite capable.'

He nodded. 'Showery Tor at six. Then we can be back well before darkness. Do you know the way?'

She nodded. 'I want to understand why you love the moor, Kitto. I want you to explain it. Just to me.'

She turned and left in a rustle and swirl of Sunday dress, heading for Arthek. Kitto gazed at her back, not feeling as warm as he should in the sunshine.

Kitto sat on Showery Tor on his favourite flat stone, with others stacked below and the moorland stretching out in all directions. The sun was fading fast and the wind was blowing stronger now. It had changed direction and was colder.

She hadn't come and he wasn't surprised. She was probably in Arthek's arms. Or behind a hovel with Talan and his strange obsidian eyes. Or dancing wildly with Jowan and Jammes. Anywhere but here. He was disappointed but was staying where he wanted to be. The pull of the moor was too strong. It always was.

The sunset was going to be extraordinary and Kitto was almost glad that Ysella was not there to share it. He knew she didn't deserve it. His flash of perception was mirrored by lightning.

He had seen sunsets hundreds of times before and marvelled at each one. He had seen dozens of thrilling storms. But never had he seen the two come together in such a spectacle of sound, speed and colour. Raindrops, the size of rhododendron buds, flattened his hair in moments. He laughed, then laughed again. Then he danced his favourite dance on his favourite stone. A wild dance, as if his limbs were barely attached. He danced till dark, bathing in the moonlight, the lightning and the rain.

Above the howling wind he heard another sound. He stopped, rubbing his eyes with the sleeve of his sodden shirt and pushing away his plastered hair. The sun had long gone. He stared. Far away, he thought he saw a light moving over Brown Willy and heading for Rough Tor at an impossible speed. He knew at once what it must be, who it must be. There was no time to think about escape or fear or excitement. Kitto was there and Woden was coming. He was as sure as he had been about anything in his life so far.

Light and movement were all around Kitto. There was snarling and gnashing, blue phosphorescence and burning red, and teeth and eyes. The storm and the Wild Hunt, inextricably joined like some mad performance.

The thunder rolled but Kitto heard the voice. 'You dance late on my moor, boy.'

So was this it? Would he be pulled slowly up the village street tomorrow, having been found broken at the bottom of Showery Tor? Poor Kitto, he must have fallen in the storm, they would say. But they would still cross themselves for protection.

'Aye, my lord, I do.'

There was no chance he would forget what Nan had taught him. He had rehearsed it a thousand times.

'Are you prepared to die?'

'If you will it, lord. But I would be your liegeman if you'll accept me.'

The thunder rolled and Kitto heard the roar of laughter in it. He looked up at the huge shifting face towering above him and that single right eye gleaming directly at him, a-fire and golden.

'Would you indeed?' The thunder stopped. The lightning flashed its last. The rain still poured. 'You know that I will give you a gift and you will be marked mine forever?'

'Aye, lord. And you will take payment too.'

'You are well informed, boy. Who is your teacher?'

'Your servant, Wenna, my nan.'

'Wenna! I recall Wenna, with her long golden tresses. A loyal servant. What is your name, boy?'

'Kitto, lord.'

'Kitto.' The deep voice rolled his name around and something stirred deep inside Kitto.

'Are you frightened of me, Kitto?'

'Yes, lord. Terrified.'

'Your honesty does you credit.'

The hounds burst into snarling and their ravening jaws came closer to Kitto. Kitto stared at them and they moved back just a fraction. Kitto held his ground.

'Brave too,' roared Woden and his steeds reared and clawed the night sky. The chariot lurched, then was almost still again. 'My hounds want to tear you to pieces. This is their hunt as well as mine.'

'If you will it, lord, so it must be. I am your servant. But would be your liegeman.'

'And so you will be, Kitto. So you will be. Prepare yourself.'

Kitto knew to kneel.

The storm grew again ferociously and Kitto was falling, spinning, and his breath was knocked out of him. His vision was filled with teeth and eyes and a sudden excruciating pain. He screamed into the screaming wind while it tore the whirlpooling air all around him. As the blackness took him, he heard the booming voice. 'You are mine!'

He woke to soothing hands on his face.

'Keep still,' came a voice. Female.

The storm had died; the moon was full and hung like a ripe silvered fruit in the sky above him. The stars were scattered and gleaming. An overpowering urge to roar came over him and he felt like dancing again. He was alive.

'Shhhhhh! You must be still.' There was a gentleness in the voice and a hint of amusement.

'Who are you?'

There was silence.

'In case you're wondering, it is I, Delen. And you needs be still while I tend your wound. And it's no use talking to me because I won't hear.'

Delen. He had known it in his heart. He smiled and relaxed on the rough moorland grass below Showery Tor and fell unconscious again.

The girl sat on a rock and watched the boy approach.

'Thank you,' said Kitto as he approached Delen.

She nodded. 'I was glad I could help.'

'It was like you were meant to be there.'

'I was.'

Kitto smiled and Delen stood up. He raised a hand to the bandage across his left eye. 'Have I lost my eye?'

'You will have lost most or all the sight from it. People will say that you stumbled and fell into thorns, even though there are no thorns where you were. Most people will need an easy explanation.'

'But we don't.'

'No. We don't.' She smiled. It was a lovely smile. Kitto smiled back.

'I had no idea that you could understand so much of what people say. You read our lips.'

She nodded. 'You are particularly easy to follow.' A pinkness appeared high on her cheekbones.

'And where did you learn your healing skills?'

'Oh, they've been with me a while.'

He nodded. 'I've seen you out collecting herbs and flowers. I think you love the moor as much as I do.'

She nodded. 'Maybe more. Have you looked at your wound yet?'

Kitto shook his head.

Her smile widened. 'Come and see.'

She led him to a small still pool at the edge of the stream then gently removed his bandage. He stooped to look into the pool, finer than any mirror. From his forehead, across his left eye and down his cheek, were three parallel marks, three vibrant raw wounds. His left eye was milky and the skin raked and puckered above it and below. But it was his other eye that made him gasp. Flecks of gold shone in the reflection.

'You are his,' whispered Delen with awe. 'You look like him now.'

'I have been accepted as his liegeman and I have paid the price. Woden will give me a gift in return.'

Delen nodded and they both stood up. Delen replaced the bandage.

They fell silent, aware of a third person approaching. Kitto heard the crunch of the pebbles and Delen looked up as she saw the shadow.

Ysella stood facing Delen and said, 'I want to speak to Kitto.' Ysella turned to Kitto. 'How do I send her away?'

'You don't,' said Kitto evenly. 'You could ask her.'

'But she's deaf.'

'Doesn't mean she can't understand things.'

Ysella looked scornfully at Delen. 'Leave us.'

Delen shook her head. 'No,' she said softly.

'What does she mean, 'no'?' said Ysella.

'She isn't your servant,' said Kitto.

Ysella looked around. Her expression had darkened and Kitto thought her less pretty.

'Please would you leave us.' Ysella still made it sound like an order but Delen wouldn't hear that. She left with a half-smile to Kitto which made Ysella scowl.

Ysella turned to face Kitto, composure restored.

'I let you down, Kitto,' she said and fluttered her eyelashes.

Kitto said nothing.

'I was busy. Didn't notice the time...'

'It's alright, Ysella. It's fine.'

She blinked. 'You mean everything can go back to normal?'

Kitto moved his head slightly from one side to the other. 'Normal?'

'Yes, the time we spend together.'

'The time,' Kitto repeated slowly.

'Yes, our friendship...' Ysella's voice petered out. Silence returned. Kitto smiled, but Ysella frowned and

Kitto could see her discomfort. Her growing desperation.

'I must go,' said Kitto.

'Please don't,' said Ysella. 'I thought we might go for a walk – perhaps on the moor.' She touched his arm and smiled.

Kitto glanced around. He could see faces watching, then turning away as his glance alighted on them. Jammes. Jowan. Arthek. Talan. All her puppets waiting to dance when Ysella said. Now Kitto understood; Ysella had lost her grip on his strings. She couldn't make him dance. She had never been interested in him. He had simply been one more local lad whose head she could turn when she wished. It was a game. Her game. For her benefit.

Kitto had changed since that night on the moor. Confidence rose further in him and he knew Ysella could sense the difference as she glanced away.

'I must go,' he said and Ysella's shoulders dropped. He felt no guilt but he did feel sorry for her. He was still the same Kitto who didn't like to hurt anyone's feelings.

Delen was sitting by the stream as Kitto approached, and turned to look at him.

'Shall we walk?' he said.

'I'd like that.'

They strolled onto the moor. The wind was blustery and cloud shadows chased over the scene before them. He found her hand; she didn't withdraw it. They turned and looked at each other. How had he ever thought her plain? She was beautiful.

'Have you always been deaf?' he asked.

'No.' She laughed, a tinkly laugh like water in a stream. He looked at her more closely. Some strands of her hair blew across his face, but his attention was taken by her eyes. The golden flecks in them shone brightly in the sunshine. And he knew. He understood. He had his gift from Woden and he gave thanks. He laughed with delight and Delen's smile lit her face.

It was more than enough. They turned and ran, hand in hand. No plans. Any direction. They ran because they could. The moor belonged to them and they belonged to the moor.

A Cornish Rant

by Anita D Hunt

A *sneak peek through a Cornish cottage window, a study in the art of the Cornish vernacular.*

'Tis no good,' Jess said as she slammed the pastry down onto the floured board. A cloud of flour ballooned from the table and slowly settled again. 'I'm gettin' sum teasy with these bleddy emmets down 'ere all the time with their upcountry ways.'

She pointed towards the bowlful of peeled potatoes that were sat on the table, 'Pass us them teddy's over will 'e maid?'

Amy did as she was bid. 'Here you go Gran. You know you really shouldn't let them get to you.'

'Aye, I knaws that, but they really get me goat and they ain't gotta clue wasson 'alf the time.'

Jess finished rolling out the pastry and started deftly

turning a large potato in one hand, chipping small bitesize chunks off with a knife before placing them in a line in the middle of the pastry.

Amy made an attempt to deflect her grandmother's temper, 'I don't know how you do that without cutting yourself.'

'Tis easy tis, jus' like drivin' down the bleddy lane is. I thought she were gonna start squallin' when she had to reverse up the 'ill. Turmits next me 'ansome.'

'It's swede Gran, turnips are white, these are yellow.'

'I'll give 'e swede! They'm all turmits to me.' She flicked the knife towards the edge of the table. 'An' if they can't drive them big cars then they shouldn't buy 'em. 'Tin't no good 'avin' 'em on our tiny roads. Beef and onion from that there bowl next.'

Amy watched as her gran dropped a dollop of butter on top of the filling, added some salt and pepper and then flipped the pastry over the top. Jess quickly crimped the edges together in a finger over thumb movement before placing it onto an opened butter wrapper on a baking sheet.

'You know, we do have greaseproof paper these days. You don't have to save all your butter wrappers anymore.'

Jess laughed, pointing her short-bladed knife and shaking her head at her granddaughter, 'I'll give 'e bleddy greaseproof paper an all! When you've bin makin' pasties longer 'un me, then you can tell us all 'bout greaseproof paper! Aye, you'm a booty you are.'

She opened the hot oven, standing back to let the burst of heat escape. Her glasses steamed up and she gave a loud 'tut' as she waited for them to clear so she could place the tray in the oven. She closed the door and knocked her glasses back into place with the back of her floury hand. Absentmindedly, she lifted the front of her gingham apron and wiped her hands.

Amy clicked the kettle into life and picked up the now cold teapot, 'Fancy a cuppa tea, Gran?'

'Aye, me cup's over there. Jus' top 'un up.'

Amy carefully tipped two teaspoonfuls of loose-leaf tea into the pot, poured the boiled water on top and placed the hand-made cosy over the top. She knew it would take at least ten minutes for the tea to stew to the perfect colour and her Gran would never accept a tea bag in a mug.

'When this pasty comes out, I'll wrap 'un up an' you can take 'un to work for your crib later.'

'Thanks Gran. You're the best. My mates are well jel of my pasties on my break.'

'What the bleddy hell is jel supposed to mean? Can't 'e talk proper English no more?'

Amy laughed. 'It means jealous Gran, they all want to pinch my lunch.'

'Well, so they bleddy well should be. Can't get better than home-made, maid. None o' that mass produced, minced up rubbish 'ere and definitely there i'nt no carrot!'

Amy smiled, nodding her head in agreement as the aroma from the cooking pasties began to fill the room. There certainly were no better pasties than those her Gran made.

'Mebbe I'll make 'e up some little ones after me cuppa. Take 'em in with 'e tomorrow and you can give 'em out to yer mates.'

She lowered her head and peered at Amy over the

top of her lenses, her forefinger wagging straight at her granddaughter.

'As long as they ain't emmets, mind!'

The White Ermine

by Froshie Evans

The tapestry opposite was moth-eaten. Ironic, as it depicted moths in its brown and grey stitching. It must have been a contemporary piece, regardless of its evident decay. It didn't look anything like the tapestries that I had seen before. I had seen lots of them, Beatrice had dragged me to enough heritage sites in the year we'd been together. Beatrice was an oddity, with her quirky librarian style, tortoiseshell glasses and a plethora of witchcraft memorabilia.

I ran a hand through my curly hair. My leg was twitching, a stimming behaviour I could never quite rid myself of. I had managed to stop biting my nails long enough to paint them a glittery dark blue, to match my navy dress and t-bar heels. Uncharacteristically feminine, but professional. I flicked through my portfolio, an action that gave me something to do with my hands rather than actually looking at it. I glanced at the sketches of beetles from my stint at the Eden Project, drawings of sea creatures, mussels and limpets, a squid here and there. Thinking about it gave me a stab of guilt; I knew it made sense for me to move here for her, but I wasn't sure I could leave my home. It gave London a grey, eerie sheen that wasn't just the smog.

An older lady, long flowing grey hair, brown birkenstocks, mustard yellow trousers and an olive green flowing top, floated past in an almost ethereal fashion. Suddenly, I worried that I appeared too professional, and not like an artist in residence should look.

'It's fine,' I muttered out loud, attempting to calm myself.

'Millie Acaster?'

A very tall, very blonde woman with a light blue shirt, black trousers and a lanyard imprinted with the museum's logo stood by the reception desk. I rose from my seat and smiled, making sure my eyes crinkled so I looked sincere.

'Hi, it's lovely to meet you. I'm Natalie. I'm head of the residency department.' She had an accent, American possibly.

'Hello, nice to meet you,' I responded.

'It says on your application you're not from London. Have you had far to come?'

We walked across the stone floor of the entrance hall, under a giant reconstruction of a white ermine moth.

'Helston, in Cornwall,' I said.

'Oh wow,' said Natalie, 'How long did that take?'

'About twelve hours, I took the overnight train.'

'Really? That's almost as long as my flight from

Vancouver.'

Canadian, not American.

We ascended the grand staircase in the centre of the room. It split off in opposite directions and we turned left. 'This might sound personal but what on earth is your perfume?' Natalie asked.

'Oh,' I laughed nervously, 'my girlfriend made me wear it. It's frankincense.'

'That's so cute. It smells gorgeous.'

'Thanks. It's a spell to protect me from evil...' I trailed off, blushing. I stole a look at my smart watch, my heartrate was at 140bpm. I was sweating; I wished I'd worn a blazer or something to cover any dampness under my arms.

'So your portfolio said you were interested in butterflies, right?' Natalie said.

'Er, yeah. Yes.' My mouth was chalky and dry. We walked along a stone corridor that was lined with a deep red carpet. I imagined a regal lady walking towards us with her maidens, perhaps a Queen.

'Well, we don't normally have many artists interested in those. Writers yes, but not artists.'

'That seems odd?' I cringed at myself for not thinking of something more intelligent to say.

'Well yeah, I thought so too. I don't know, people might think it's cliché or something.' Natalie said it without accusation, but I could feel my face burning.

'Well, I was hoping to do projects on all sorts of insects and-'

'Oh no,' Natalie interrupted, 'I don't think they're cliché, not at all. My masters research was in the migration pattern of the monarch butterfly across Mexico.'

'Oh, fascinating!' I said. And I meant it.

We reached a large wooden door. It had large metal hinges that looked like spears stabbing into the dark panels. 'The lab is through that door,' Natalie said.

I motioned for her to go first.

'Oh no, I'm not going in. The writer in residence is in there to talk to you one on one.'

My heart leapt into my throat.

'Besides,' Natalie continued, 'the West tower is super creepy.'

'Well, I like creepy,' I joked, then cringed again.

Natalie frowned for a brief moment but didn't comment.

'His name is Jeffrey. He's really chatty so don't be nervous,' she said.

I opened the medieval door; it creaked ominously.

It's just nerves, I told myself. Not everything is something sinister.

I ascended a small spiral staircase, the door clanking shut behind me. It was stuffy. It smelled like an old book, usually a welcome scent. It now made the hairs on the back of my neck prickle.

The stairs opened into a large circular room, I could just about make out a black and yellow tiled floor. It was dark, the kind of grey like in the moments before sunrise. I wasn't alone. A scuffling sound from the other side of the room made my hair stand on end.

I cleared my throat, but the scuffling didn't stop. I was acutely aware of a faint monotonous buzzing.

'Jeffrey?' I called. The sound was muffled, as if the walls were covered in sound insulation, even though I could clearly see the stonework even in the duskiness. I looked up and noticed the ceiling was made of glass, as if it was meant to be a garden room. Each pane of glass was covered with yellowed paper and tape to block out the sun. A shadow appeared behind one of the rows of cabinets on the far side of the room.

'Yes?' the shadow hissed.

'I'm Millie, for the artist in residence interview?'

'And?' the voice replied. It was a higher pitch than I had expected, though not feminine at all. Natalie was right, the room was creepy, and so was Jeffrey. He stumbled about, knocking glass trinkets that clinked together. My eyes had adjusted to the darkness but I still couldn't make him out.

'I was told you wanted to talk one to one, perhaps about my project? I thought we could collabo-'

'I'm not interested,' he hissed and skulked out of sight.

I was taken aback. I wanted this job. No, I needed this job. For Beatrice, to support Beatrice, I repeated to myself.

'You haven't seen my portfolio yet,' I said, making sure my voice didn't waver.

'Where are you from?' said Jeffrey, still hiding.

'Cornwall.' There was that flash of homesickness again; perhaps that was why I felt so uneasy.

The buzzing sound came to an abrupt stop, just for a moment. It resumed when Jeffrey started talking. I felt uncomfortable, like when a big black fly is trapped inside a room and bangs into the window over and over.

'Kernow?' said Jeffrey. 'What do you eat in Kernow?'

I was perplexed. 'Pasties? Jam? Those stodgy cakes? The beige ones with raisins sometimes,' Jeffrey hissed.

'S-scones?' I stuttered, not because I was scared, but because the air was heavy. I felt as though I couldn't breathe. I had begun to pant, a precursor to a panic attack. 'Yesss' Jeffrey hissed. 'That will make you look very sweet.'

He appeared to the right, making a wet, smacking sound with his lips. I stepped back. My heel crunched on something papery.

'And clotted cream?' he hissed again. I could see he was hunched over, but even stooped he was sarcastically tall, almost cartoonish. I would have laughed if he hadn't been so frightening. His face was long, almost glowing.

'Oh yes.' With every step back towards the stairs I took, he lurched closer. 'We have a farm with Jersey Cows. Their milk makes the cream.'

'Oooh, such an excellent addition you will make.' He clapped his hands together in delight; his glee revealed a scar along his cheek bone that cracked open like a vertical grimace. His mustard yellow eyes rolled into the back of his head.

'Yesss,' he said with a menacing glare. 'Utterly delightful.'

I remembered Beatrice at home, looking through the museum website, saying that the writer in residence was barely older than me, that he had sandy blonde hair and could pass for a teenager. My stomach sank while I gazed into the demonic face of the stranger in front of me.

'Where is Jeffrey?' I whispered.

'Oh my dear, why don't you come look?'

He scooped a long, spindly arm around my shoulder and ushered me away from the stairs. I tried to resist but he was so much stronger. He lead me to a cabinet at the far side of the room. It was taller than both of us with thin horizontal drawers in two columns. Not-Jeffrey pushed me forward towards it,

'Check the drawers,' he growled in my ear.

'He's dead?' I cried, adrenaline coursed through my veins; my heart beat so fast I thought it would burst.

'No, he's not dead. I am not a killer, I am a collector.'

He gently pushed me again and I reached out with shaking hands. I picked a drawer at random and opened it. Afraid to look inside, I screwed my eyes shut.

'Look, girl, it's not frightening,' said not-Jeffrey, his tone softer.

I opened one eye, then the other. A butterfly had flown from the drawer. Its silver wings fluttered in the dank air, searching for light. I opened another drawer; this time two took flight. That's when I saw it; they weren't butterflies. They were moths. I pulled drawers at random in sharp, frantic movements. Some slid open with ease, others were stuck and needed a forceful tug. All of them contained moths who flew around the air above us searching for light and freedom. Not-Jeffrey was jumping about in a sort of jig. It was almost charming, the way he flapped his arms and swung his legs, trying to jump as if to join them dancing in the air.

I pulled the last drawer, the drawer in the middle with the ruby handle, but no moth flew out of it. It was empty. An almighty crack sounded and for a split second, the moths were jostled. The cabinet split down the middle and opened out to reveal a chamber hidden within it. There was a single gleam of natural light bearing down like a spotlight on a stage. It landed on the centre of a glass container, long and cylindrical, six foot tall but two foot wide. It contained a single moth, flapping its wings in a futile attempt at escape.

'It's nearly ready, but not quite,' said not-Jeffrey, all the jauntiness from moments ago forgotten.

'What do you mean?' I asked.

'Look again, girl.'

My gaze followed the moth, flying up frantically, and floating down slowly, sadly. It landed on top of a heap of old clothes at the base of the jar. I was filled with melancholy, my heart and stomach felt heavy. I imagined it crying, the sound so strong in my mind I could almost hear it for real. I sobbed; as I wiped a tear from my chin I realised the crying was me. The moth took flight again, but couldn't get the same altitude as before. I was transfixed. I edged closer to the killing jar. The heap of clothes shuddered as the moth rose higher.

'Jeffrey?' I whispered.

I gasped as I realised; he was the pile of clothes. He was the moth.

A ripping sound behind me broke my focus as the horrible figure who had tormented me tore out of his clothes, hump first. Only it wasn't a hump at all. It was beautiful white wings speckled with black polka dots, and as he stretched them out they covered the chamber entrance entirely. His snow white body was covered in a thick fur, tufted around his neck like the coat of a thrice divorced socialite. He clawed at his human face with the scar and tore it off with one of his six furry limbs. Two jet black feathers stood erect atop his head. He was beautiful, but he was dangerous. He lunged at me. I ducked out of his way. He crashed into the killing jar, smashing it to pieces. The tiny moth flew through the cabinet and joined the others in the rush to find freedom.

I ran after him, clumsy in the shoes I wasn't used to. I grabbed the nearest object, a lepidopterology encyclopaedia. I launched it at the ceiling with both hands, like a hammer thrower. It smashed through the glass, tearing through the paper coverings. The swarm of moths disappeared into the golden light.

A screech from behind curdled my blood, the hair on my arms stood on end.

'My collection!' it screamed. 'What did you do?'

I ran, but the monster took flight, its wings beating the air so hard it knocked me to the ground. It swooped down, its six legs extended ready to grab me. I scrambled unsuccessfully, my dress restricted my movements, my shoes slipped on the smooth floor. Its feet were directly above me, I screamed as it flapped its wings again. I covered my face with my arms; I felt a gentle stroke on my wrist, but heard it screech and flap away. The frankincense spell! It was all the time I needed to crawl towards the stairs. I threw myself down them horizontally, tumbling round and down until I thudded against the door. The monster was too big to fit through the stairwell but it was coming for me all the same. I clawed at the door, its feathery antennae inches away from me, until finally the door opened and I landed in the hallway in a heap on the floor. I crawled away from the moth immediately and pulled myself up. I ran, my heels clip clip clipping against the floor. No one was there.

Natalie, I thought, with a stab of anger. Natalie must

have known.

I fled down the next staircase which led to the grander one in the abandoned entrance room and I ran, faster than I had ever before. I stumbled, my ankle twisting, but I ran on, past the empty reception desk, past the tapestry of the creature I was running from, through the glass fronted doors and finally...

I was outside, panting heavily. I turned to face the building I had just run out of, but it had vanished. In its place, metal fences with a construction sign hanging from the railings. My heart was still thumping in my chest as I peered through the gap between the fences. It was all gone, just scattered piles of rubble, a JCB with some men in orange high-vis jackets and dusty white hard hats. The building was gone, and so was the threat.

I took a deep steadying breath. I walked towards the real museum opposite, feeling as if I wasn't quite touching the ground. I smoothed my hair and entered the building. It was the same inside: the bench I had sat on, the reception desk, a huge insect hanging in the entrance hall. There was one difference; there was no moth-eaten tapestry staring at me from across the room.

My bag and portfolio were still waiting for me. I took a seat and opened the sketchbook. A tiny moth fluttered out and landed on my forefinger.

'Hey Jeffrey, it's a pleasure to meet you,' I murmured to him. He batted his wings as if in response.

Out of the corner of my eye, I noticed a short boy around my age, with sandy hair and a pen behind his ear. He was deep in conversation with a very tall woman with very blonde hair, and from what I could tell, a Canadian accent. The woman checked her watch, frowning.

'Perhaps,' I said to the moth on my finger. 'Perhaps we should go back home.'

There is Copper in Abundance

by Ulrike Duran

Sampson Waters was born 1805 in Scorrier. He made his fortune in the mining industry in South America. He returned to Cornwall in 1860 and saw out his life in Gyllyndune House in Falmouth.

Copiapó, Chile 1839

Dear Peggy,

How have you and the children been in the last months? What news is there from home? Has the church window been repaired? Aunt Cornelia – has she recovered? Does John still like collecting woodlice? And Mary, does she still suck her thumb? And did Uncle Henry help you control that beastly ivy - I hope it's not still blocking the kitchen window?

It has only been three months, and already home is

starting to feel like a faded dream. I miss your smile and the children's voices. By the time you receive this letter, another three months will have passed and when I read your reply another three – so nine months. Like waiting for our babies. I cannot imagine being apart for this long. Will you not change your mind and join me?

The journey to Chile was more arduous than I expected. The cabins were small but relatively comfortable. However, it was the storm that raged and played with the ship as if it were a rocking horse that caused most of the crew to be as sick as dogs. Later we had some days of extreme heat, where the sun scorched our skins, not just with the rays from above but also from the reflection of the water.

Despite all this, there were some magical things to be seen along the way that you also would have loved. Get the map out while you read this to the children, so they can see what I'm talking about. A school of dolphins followed us along the coast of Argentina; and when we sailed up the Magellan Strait we saw the impressive blue whale, a creature almost as big as our ship. When I saw its huge tail swing up above the water, I felt small and yet closer to God than ever before. Children, I suggest you re-read the story of Jonah and the Whale and think of your father in the presence of such a powerful sea-creature. Then we sailed around Cape Horn, right at the bottom of South America, and some natives waved at us, naked, painted in stripes. Later I was told they are called the Selknam people. Also, penguins – funny little black and white birds that cannot fly but swim like seals – were nesting on the islands just off the mainland there.

Arriving in Chile, we landed in a port called Valparaiso – the valley of paradise. Like Falmouth, it is a harbour with colourful houses, except here the colours are bright and almost shouting at you. Very pretty to see when you first approach. Once landed it is quite different though. It is a typical big port with grimy roads, where people try to sell you everything and anything. Mules and horses and carriages and people all scramble along the roads; pickpockets and prostitutes lurk in the corners. It does have charming Spanish style houses and some impressive naval buildings. On the squares, some locals play pan-pipes and you can get your shoes shined. One of the squares has a small statue of Romulus and Remus with their wolf-mother. This would be another good story to read for the children: the founding of Rome. To reach the hills where wealthy people have built their houses, you have to climb steep steps or cobbled roads. I can see why: the views over the Pacific are immense. Everything here is more intense, bigger and chaotic. This a country of enormous landscape, so vast and huge are the skies, the plains and the mountains. Even the Pacific Ocean seems wilder than the Atlantic on our coast. They say this is the last country God made, using left-overs of everywhere.

We did not stay in Valparaiso; we soon travelled to the capital, Santiago, before heading north to Copiapó. Santiago is as I imagine Paris: sophisticated, fashionable, cultured. I am sure you would have enjoyed staying there for longer, which many of the wives did. The women here wear the finest gowns: silks and pearls are easy to come by. How I would love to see them on you in real life and not just in my mind.

Copiapó itself is a town surrounded by mountains and desert. The houses are single storied and there is a church in the middle. There is a square where people have tried to grow trees for shade. The church looks like it will need repair soon and I thought of your efforts for our church at home. There are plenty of Cornish here for company, but the community is mixed with locals. Mostly miners, but some of ours have settled with Chilean wives. They would love your resourcefulness here. It will be important for me to learn the local language, Spanish, if I want to get ahead in business. I think you would laugh at my attempts at pronouncing these new words!

It is a barren landscape and nothing much grows – what would your green fingers advise? Beyond the mountains, there are dunes of sand that carry on and on with no end. A local miner, who has lived here his whole life, told us he has never seen the rain. Men travel on mules on roads that are hard to see yet they seem to know where they're going. I have seen both men and mules, dead on the roadside due to the heat. It's a gruesome sight. Maybe you wouldn't have enjoyed it here. Maybe you were right not to come. For entertainment there is cock and bull-fighting on a Sunday but don't worry, your brother and I invest our money in mining not fights.

When I agreed to come to Chile with your brother to work for the Copiapó Mining Company, I had hoped that I wouldn't have to write a letter like this. I know you don't like boats (I well remember how sick you felt on our trip along the Helford). Of course, you want to stay close to your mother too and I can hardly imagine the village coping without your continuous efforts. So I understand why, but I can't help feeling disappointed. I had as much choice in crossing the Atlantic as I had in going down the mines in the first place. It is our family's way of life: we follow the money. But you know all that.

As I said, there was never any choice in this. Not if I were to make any more of myself and therefore our family. I never did like going down the mines. Not now. Not all those years ago. It was supposed to be natural to me, father being a miner and all; all the men we knew in the village too. I was used to the sounds and the smells of the engines and furnaces; I had been by the site plenty a time. But when it came to going underground for the first time, that was something different. I was excited in the morning, and mother gave me a good hug and a pasty to put in my pocket and a 'Take care, will you, my love.' She turned and said to Father, 'Make sure you look after our Sampson here,' and he nodded and scratched the back of his neck. I remember it like it were yesterday, I do. I felt all grown up walking to work with Father in the morning. He never spoke much, and he didn't say much that morning neither. No explaining. So when we reached the site, I was bundled along with all the others. I was supposed to know what to do already. I looked up at Father, and as though he read my thoughts, he said, 'You'll learn as you go along, son.' But as we reached the opening of the mine shaft, my legs stopped working for what felt like minutes, until one of the men said gruffly, 'Come on boy, there's work to be done.' I had no choice. I was shoved in with the others. Once down there, I felt like I couldn't breathe, but there wasn't time to think about it. I was put straight to work. I copied Father and he showed me how to use the tools. Clang clang, puff

puff, whistle whistle. Those sounds still follow me today, even if the mines here are quiet. Here no smoke, furnaces or great steam-engines disturb the solitude of the desert and mountains.

Finally, there was a break and I dug out mother's pasty from my pocket, still a bit warm inside. Sitting in that mine, it was the most comforting, peppery, more turnip-than-meat pasty I had ever tasted. It made it better somehow, being in that dark stuffy tunnel. I am grateful that you learnt how to make them from her, as they were always a comfort to me. Here, would you believe it, they have their own version of pasty that they call empanada. They are filled with meat too, and onion, but no turnip nor potato. They have a boiled egg inside and raisins and olives. A strange tasting concoction, being savoury and sweet at the same time. But it is growing on me already, even after just a few weeks.

Like we discussed before I left, I cannot make this kind of fortune in Cornwall. It is here, where there is more copper and silver and opportunity than ever imaginable at home. I can become someone here. You see, the reason these mines are so quiet is not because they use the cheapest form of mining. It is because they throw the ore away, thinking it to be worthless, when in fact it is the richest vein. They even laughed at us for buying it (when it is us who are really laughing). I'm telling you, there is a fortune to be made here. We have also rescued scoria and slag from some old furnaces and sent mules to carry these cinders to the coast for transport to England. Another strange thing is that the natives are afraid of the safety fuse. So, as you can see, there is much work to be done here, and much hope. There is copper in abundance and I am hoping to find silver.

Much love to you and the children. It makes me smile, imagining you reading my news by our hearth in the cottage, the fire warming your feet. Enclosed you will find instructions on how to access the accounts. I know you will use it wisely, on the family and the community.

I do look forward to news from Cornwall.

God Bless,

Yours, Sampson.

A Spell in Cornwall

by Claudia Loveland

'Tragic magic.' 'Plasma miasma.' Tantalising phrases swirled in his semi-consciousness. 'Empirical miracle.' 'The dynamics of physics dispelled by the spells of psychics.' He must intrigue his audience on Wednesday night. 'Illusion confusion.' He had to hook them. 'Laws of logic mauled in the maws of mystery.'

Al became aware that he was awake – and that it was Wednesday.

He turned to look at Belle beside him, so close, so detached. Beautiful in the half-light. He reached across to touch her and she pushed back against the pressure. He slid his fingers into the curve of her neck. She didn't react. Maybe she'd slipped into sleep at exactly that moment. He often woke as she was settling down. He eased his middle-aged body out of bed and did his morning stretches.

He looked out over the garden, colourless in the spring dawn. His gaze fell on the long, hollowed-out granite block, half buried, beside the hedge. He'd heard its story before he'd moved into the cottage a couple of years earlier. This was the trough that had saved the life of St Kea, on his way to Cornwall in the Dark Ages. His boat had sunk in a storm, but a cattle trough had floated towards him on the waves. It had carried him onwards, around the coast, up the river, and safely to the shore.

In this pale light, the legend was almost believable. Looking down the hill, over the rooftops and the fields, he could see the line of the creek marked out by a ribbon of mist hanging above it.

He left Belle to sleep. She was almost nocturnal these days.

In the kitchen, he chopped some fruit to add to his muesli. At this hour, he often heard his mother's voice. For her last eighteen months, he'd got her up and made breakfast. Smoothies were all she could manage.

'You will move to Cornwall when I've gone, won't you, dear?' Her voice had been weak. 'Sell this place. Find somewhere nice. Somewhere with a view. Somewhere you can make friends.'

He understood.

She managed a smile, 'You're still tall, dark and handsome.'

He'd admit to each of those, but that wasn't the point. And anyway, five foot eleven wasn't really tall.

At the end, she could barely whisper. 'A fresh start. Make the most of it.'

It had been such a good death. She'd often said her faith would hold her up; she'd be ready to go. Was there a spiritual streak in the family? Could a genetic predisposition account for his new obsession with the Cornish mystics? He'd spend the morning rehearsing his talk. Then he'd rest; recharge for the evening. 'Three p's,' he smiled to himself. Preparation, Practice, Put-your-feet-up.

He did a complete run-through. Twice. But his mind resisted an after-lunch nap, musing on the way things had turned out. He'd been surprised how many clubs there were, all looking for entertaining speakers to bolster their bar takings. The events had given him some recognition locally, and useful contacts. Was he more creative than he'd thought? He wasn't very imaginative and was probably low on emotional intelligence – everyone said so, anyway – but he was enjoying his life's new focus.

He wondered what his former colleagues would think of him now. Most had envied his early-retirement. Ten years early. Some, though, had viewed the move as risky for someone like him. 'Alan, you've improved the lives of so many people,' his boss had said, 'and you haven't had to actually meet any of them.'

Exactly. She'd sized him up, but she was wrong if she reckoned he didn't like people. Enzymes were more interesting, of course, but he'd always been on good terms with the rest of his department. He'd avoided promotion too, after a while. No point in having to manage anyone. That could become tricky. But so long as his colleagues didn't interrupt his research, they were fine.

'You've got a good crowd here already,' he said to the club chairman as he arrived. He was relieved that someone had been at the door, looking out for him. 'How many are you expecting?'

'Oh, a fair number.' The chairman led him to a table at the front of the hall. 'For a talk like yours, we get all sorts, not just the older ones. They'll come from a distance too.' He nodded to a woman with bright, yellow hair, who was smiling at them from across the room. 'She's not one of our regulars. Only comes when she's interested. Phoebe something-or-other. Unusual woman.' He looked at his watch. 'Right. Anything else you need? A drink?'

At the bar, Al noticed the woman again. She didn't appear particularly unusual – apart from the hair. Quite good-looking.

He felt buoyant. He considered attempting his only useful phrase in Cornish: 'Yeghes da!' – 'Good health!' He hadn't had the confidence to try it so far.

Later, at home, he decided it had been his best presentation yet. It was sure to result in more bookings. He'd scarcely glanced at his notes. At the end, the woman with the yellow hair had waylaid him, and they'd talked for an hour and twenty minutes. She'd known a lot about the legends, but not the medieval sources or the eighth-century texts. They'd arranged to discuss those on Monday night. He'd look forward to that; maybe draft a brief outline for her.

Belle wasn't interested, of course, but he told her about it anyway. He'd come to see the value of verbal processing.

He wished he'd worked harder at conversation over

the years. He still didn't approve of talking for the sake of talking – and besides, he didn't know how to do it – but things might have been easier with girlfriends. It had been good with Lynette, though. They'd met at work and understood each other. 'It's our chemistry that gives us a bond,' she used to say. He liked that line. Things had been going well. He'd thought about marriage.

'I'm sorry, Al. I seem to have said this so often, but I don't really know how else to put it. I just need more. More of you.' They were in the kitchen – their kitchen – in the West London flat. 'I can't hang around any longer. It feels like I've wasted four years of my life – four years of your life – hoping you'd change. Somehow. But I don't think you can. It's not fair of me to expect you to.'

It hadn't been a waste of his time.

She was kind. She was the one who'd suggested he had some counselling. But had he accepted the therapist's views too readily? Could a label explain him?

Belle had wandered off. She reminded him of a wraith from ancient folklore. Completely autonomous. Liberated. Which suited them both.

On Monday evening, he was half an hour early for his meeting about the manuscripts. They'd agreed on a pub with 'atmosphere,' and he chose a corner table where he could watch people coming in. Sitting with his laptop open, he spotted a typing error. Not what he expected of himself. Annoying. He started to rework his next two paragraphs. He didn't notice her until she slid into the chair beside him, with a large glass of white wine in one hand.

'Have a look.' He pushed his laptop sideways. 'I've made this clearer.' She looked confused. 'Some notes for you. I'll send you a copy.'

'Okay. Thanks.' She was smiling.

He talked her through all the earliest material, and she connected it with a couple of local tales that were new to him. She kept leaning in closer to see the screen.

'Right,' he said, when he reached the end of his notes. 'I don't think there's much else I can tell you.' He closed his laptop and slid it into its case.

She shifted her chair away from him, but only a little. 'So, what now?' She nudged her empty glass towards the centre of the table.

'Well, the British Library may have some material hidden away. I'm not going there, though, until I've worked through what's already available. Then, maybe, another doctorate.' He stretched back in his chair. 'So, I'll push off now. I hope that's been useful. I've enjoyed talking it through.'

He had.

He thought about his future research. Maybe he'd need a research assistant. Should he mention that? It seemed premature – and she was asking him something about his car.

'The car? It's in the car park. I'll leave it there while I get some milk from the corner shop,' he said.

They didn't say much more as they parted. She moved off towards the bar, or perhaps she was just going to the ladies'.

He changed his mind about the milk. There was probably enough at home.

In the car, he checked his phone and replied to an email. As he drove away, he caught sight of her, coming out of the pub. He gave her a wave, but didn't think she saw him. He realised he was beginning to relax with people. He might be making friends. Perhaps Phoebe would be a friend. She'd mentioned training as a nurse in London. He felt drawn. He'd look out for her. She'd be easy enough to spot, with that hair. There was something different about her. Phoebe. She'd introduced herself as Phoebs, but he couldn't quite bring himself to call her that.

'Hey! You're here.'

It was Thursday. He was in his local pub and Phoebe was striding towards him. The light evenings matched his mood, so he'd picked up his laptop and walked down into the village – early enough to claim the table in the far corner. He stood up, barging the table; it screeched on the wooden floor. She didn't sit down.

'I was hoping I'd bump into you,' she said. 'Greg at the club said you lived round here, and this is the only pub for miles, so I popped in on Tuesday. Terry behind the bar said he knew you. Said you live in the last cottage up the hill, but hardly ever come in here.' It sounded as though she'd have come knocking on his window. 'But here you are.'

'I've never been stalked before.'

'I'm not stalking you. I was cross with you, though. Driving away like that.'

'I was going home.'

'But we agreed we'd meet outside, at your car.'

'I said I was going to buy some milk.'

'Yeah – to give me time to pop into the loo and then

come and join you.'

'No. No, no... You...'

Phoebe was laughing. He was making an odd noise in the back of his throat. People were staring.

'Can I buy you a drink?' His voice was working again. 'Let's sit down and talk.'

But no, she had to go. She'd only popped in on the off-chance, though she would like to talk. Yes, she really would like it if they could talk. A proper chat. They settled on Saturday morning, at the pub, for coffee.

She left, and he dropped back onto his chair and pulled the table towards him. The people who'd been watching had looked away already.

Terry-behind-the-bar came over, collecting empty glasses.

'You've met our Phoebs then. There's no harm in her.'

'Er?'

'Phoebs – our local witch. Didn't you know? Does charms and things. Spells, perhaps. She's alright, though.' He put the empties down on the table and leant across. 'This'll sound weird to you – you're a scientist or something, aren't you? – but when my Annie's leg swelled up, the doctors were clueless. Phoebs's ointment brought the swelling down nicely. Maybe just a coincidence. Maybe not.'

Next morning, he woke early, wanting it to be Saturday. Oh well. Tomorrow. Tomorrow, if he walked down to the pub, she might offer him a lift home. If she came in for a while... His mind roved around the cottage. Laboratory-clean, but was it inviting? Somewhere, he had a large scented candle, a retirement present. And he'd buy a pot plant for the front room. Just in case.

He went downstairs, and was surprised by the mess. Smears of mud on the kitchen floor trailed back to a wet, crumpled leaf and some grass, by the cat-flap.

'Belle? Have you got a present for me?'

She dropped something dark and flabby at his feet and tiptoed away to wash her paws.

He sighed, bent down, and picked up the shrew by its tail. As he straightened, it startled him by wriggling, but he kept his hold, and it slumped again. Supporting its body on his other forearm, he elbowed his way out of the back door.

Crouching beside the hedge, he eased the shrew onto the ground behind the saint's granite trough. It didn't move.

Alive, but playing safe? He could understand that.

'Go on, little one. A fresh start. Make the most of it.'

The shrew seemed to tense, then it skittered into the undergrowth.

'Yeghes da,' he said. 'Yeghes da.'

Stargazy Pie in the Sky
a Cornish Romp!
by Pen King

A comedy depicting the collision of two different worlds.

Cast:

PEN: *40ish, the storyteller. An observer, moves the action along, stays seated.*

MR EMMET: *30ish. A wealthy businessman from London.*

MRS EMMET: *30ish. His sweet patient well-spoken wife.*

LOWENNA: *20. A young intelligent landlady with a mischievous sense of humour and broad Cornish accent.*

LITTLE EMMETS: *Twins, young primary school age.*

GRANDPA NANCARROW: *80ish. A typical elderly Cornish man.*

SPEAKING SEAGULL.

TRISTAN: 20ish. *A young garage attendant.*

Grandpa Nancarrow, the speaking seagull and Tristan are played by the same actor.

*Sketch 1 - **In the BMW**. **Midday**.*
Chairs arranged as in a car: Mr & Mrs Emmet at front, twin
Emmets at back. Grandpa Nancarrow is standing looking over
his gate centre stage smoking his pipe. Pen on stool at one side.

PEN: Mr and Mrs Emmet and their two little Emmets arrive at the beginning of the summer season, intending to stay for the full six weeks at Fowey. What can possibly go wrong?

GRANDPA NANCARROW: Foweee ... *(He shakes his head. A slow smile spreads across his wrinkles.)* Now let me zee... *(He draws on his pipe.)* You goes along 'ere, ignore sat-nav, then 'tis either turn to the right or *(He leans on his wooden gate.)* 'tis on the left.

MR EMMET: I've already endured the A30 with that stupid dual carriageway. What idiot designed those single lanes?

LITTLE EMMETS: We want the beach, want beach!

MRS EMMET: I read in the paper, the council are fixing all this. You'll be pleased to know they've begun widening the lanes.

MR EMMET: So some clot thought it would be a good idea to start the work in the middle of summer!

GRANDPA NANCARROW: Now look ee 'ere young man! Don't ee go bringing your up-country grouchiness down 'ere.

LITTLE EMMETS: Ice-cream. Ice-cream!

MR EMMET: And these winding lanes, not one signpost to be seen!

GRANDPA NANCARROW: Uz farmers have our ways...

MR EMMET: And your hedges need cutting back.

GRANDPA NANCARROW: Our hedges hide the rock solid boundaries of our county so you'd best take care.

MR EMMET: Don't you tell me how to drive!

(The Emmets make sounds of a car brrrming away.)

PEN: Mr Emmet is unaware of the make-up of a Cornish hedge. Will he find out?

Sketch 2 - In the kitchen at the B & B. Early afternoon. The Emmet family are sat around a table. Mr Emmet has his map. Mrs Emmet has changed into her pale blue outfit.

PEN: The Emmets have arrived at last in Fowey and checked in at Treth Krowji.

(Enter Lowenna stage left.)

LOWENNA: I'll give ee some advice; first off, Mowzle. 'Tis a great place, the harbour beach is sandy, good for twins. Have a look on your map.

(Mr Emmet studies his map.)

MR EMMET: I see no trace of Mowzle. And I don't want sand in my Rolex.

MRS EMMET: Never mind dear, don't groan!

MR EMMET: I've decided we'll head out for a cream tea.

LITTLE EMMETS: Bye bye. Bye bye Lowenna!

(Lights dim to blackout.)

LOWENNA: *(Looks after her 'disappearing' guests, then speaks to her audience.)* Six weeks here! They'll be knowing a few of our three hundred beaches. Beautiful they are!

Sketch 3 - In the BMW, static in a Cornish lane, late afternoon.
Chairs arranged as in a car with 2 at front, 2 at back.

PEN: The Emmets have come to a halt behind a herd of sheep.

(Baa-ing noises off stage by Lowenna!)
LITTLE EMMET 1: *(Looking out of the car window.)* Sheeps! Woolly sheeps!
(Mr Emmet keeps his cool as Mrs Emmet spies a pasty shop.)
MRS EMMET: Ignore the sheep, children. Look dearest, pasties. What a find!
(Mr Emmet pulls on the handbrake. His wife jumps out of the car and joins a long queue. Mr Emmet waits, fingers tapping on the steering wheel.)
LITTLE EMMET 2: Look look, birdies! Lots birdies!
(Seagull noises off stage by Lowenna!)
(Mr Emmet sighs loudly, tutting as he turns off the ignition.)
MR EMMET: Those birdies are thieves! Thieves living on a diet of pasties and ice cream.
(Mr Emmet swings the keys on his finger in an annoyed manner. Eventually Mrs Emmet emerges from the pasty shop.)
MRS EMMET: Here we are darlings!
MR EMMET: *(Opening the car door.)* Look out! Those seagulls aren't scared of you! They care about one thing only and that's our pasties. Quick, hand them over.
(Mr Emmet takes a pasty from his wife.)
SEAGULL: Now... in for the kill!

PEN: Mr Emmet was holding his pasty but where is it now?

(Mrs Emmet jumps into the car before any further thieving can take place.)
MR EMMET: Hey! *(He shakes his fist at the seagull.)* You won't get away with that.
MRS EMMET: Now sweethearts, don't drop any crumbs in Daddy's nice car.
MR EMMET: Thieving machines they are. Let's get out of this sheep jam!

PEN: They head back to Treth Krowji in the mizzle, that special rain which only happens in Cornwall.

Sketch 4 The B & B kitchen, early evening.
Mr Emmet standing. The other Emmets are seated on chairs around a table with Lowenna.

LOWENNA: *(With a bright smile.)* You'll learn proper reversing down here. In our country lanes you'll often have a tractor or two in front of you.
MR EMMET: And a herd of silly sheep. And I know how to drive. I've been driving a long time.
LOWENNA: I can see that Mr Emmet. You must be very old!

PEN: Be careful Lowenna! He's worn quite well!

LOWENNA: Just remember things are done at our pace, a Cornish pace. Dreckly!
MR EMMET: Last advice you gave me was about a non-existent place called Mowzle. *(He stares out the window. Growling.)* Dreadful weather.

113

LOWENNA: Ah. *(She winks at a little Emmet.)* Cornish weather... Mizzle, like Mowzle. You muzt learn 'ow to speak! Mowzle is Mouse Hole, like Foy is Fowee. Of course!

MR EMMET: *(With sarcasm.)* Of course. *(He beams.)* And your silly place names like Praze-an-Beeble, and Polyphant ... whoever heard of anything so ridiculous. We're from Chelsea, you know.

MRS EMMET: *(She pats her husband's arm soothingly.)* Calm down darling.

MR EMMET: *(He glares at Lowenna.)* Those names are set up to confuse us... Ventongimps! *(He shakes his head in disbelief.)*

LOWENNA: Mr Emmet...call me Lowenna...would you like a cream tea?

PEN: Mr Emmet is taken aback by Lowenna's offer. His day had been anything but a holiday. First day of six weeks, it didn't bear thinking about.

(Lowenna pulls up a chair for him and he plonks himself down.)

LOWENNA: Make yourself comfortable, be with you dreckly! *(Lowenna exits stage left.)*

PEN: She is back within a minute, bustling around him with a clatter of plates.

LOWENNA: *(Enters stage left with cream tea.)* When having cream tea, it's jam first. Proper job.

(Lowenna mischievously places a pot of Rodda's clotted cream

on the table by the twins. Seeing an opportunity, the children dip their fingers into the cream and lick them!)
LITTLE EMMETS: Yummy, yummy!

PEN: Lowenna pats the dandruff from Mr. Emmet's collar, and winks again at the baby Emmets.

LOWENNA: Royt 'ansum your daddy be!
(Mrs Emmet glares)
LOWENNA: *(Bobbing a little curtsey.)* Night me luverrr!
(She leaves the room stage left.)

PEN: *(Downton Abbey music from the trailer can be heard.)* It's too early to turn in so they switch the TV on and watch the aristocratic family life of the Downton Abbey Estate. Surely they are mentally noting who is wearing what, and certainly Mr Emmet would like a butler, a chauffeur and several servants on his staff! Soon the little Emmets fall asleep.

(Mr and Mrs Emmet carry the sleeping children out, stage right. Mrs Emmet can be heard singing a lullably.)

PEN: Mrs Emmet pops them into bed, and while her husband strolls in the garden puffing on his Henri Winterman cigar, she unpacks his clothes and hangs them neatly in the wardrobe. I observe his Ray-Ban sunglasses on the bedside table. Nothing but the best!

Sketch 5 - The B & B Kitchen, early morning.
Table with 4 chairs around.

(Emmet family enter stage left.)

PEN: Next morning Mr Emmet makes an entrance all dressed up in his posh togs; a new Gucci Tshirt and matching designer shorts. Unfortunately no-one is in the kitchen to applaud! He is looking for breakfast.

MR EMMET: Lowenna has obviously overslept.

PEN: The B&B is silent. But no! The front door opens with a clatter of her surf board and Lowenna enters in her wetsuit, surprising them.

LOWENNA: *(Enters clumsily stage right with surfboard.)* Zurf's up!

MR EMMET: Is that any reason for being late?

MRS EMMET: My husband is not happy to start day two like this.

LOWENNA: Zurfs up is reason for anything! Early to bed, early to rise, that's me! *(Exits stage left.)*

(The Emmets sit at the table. Mrs Emmet reading the Times. Mr Emmet looking at his map.)

PEN: Breakfast is good, sunny side up. It is Lowenna's 21st birthday. She is extra happy!

LOWENNA: *(Enters stage left with 4 plates balanced on her arm.)* Where you be off to today? Rowter lies atop Bodmin Moor. The mizzle's lifted so there'll be a good view. Take your Canon camera.

MR EMMET: Actually it's a Panasonic Lumix GH5.

MRS EMMET: *(Smiling at Lowenna.)* Rowter?

LOWENNA: Rowter, Rough Tor to you. Could be a few tourists up there doing traffic jams in style. *(She laughs.)* I could tell ee a few stories...

MRS EMMET: Oh, we love stories, don't we sweetheart?

MR EMMET: Do we? First I knew of it!

LOWENNA: *(With a broad smile at the Baby Emmets, whispering loudly.)* Stories about smuggler's pubs, where the food's hanging ready for aliens driving around in Gucci flip-flops! Better watch out, you'll slam into something....

MR EMMET: *(Interrupts with a loud sigh.)* hhhhh...like a Cornish hedge?

LOWENNA: *(Putting on her best posh accent.)* Well, have a nice day! Actually I'm dining at the Nare!

MRS EMMET: *(Mr & Mrs Emmet exchange surprised looks.)* We'll go to the beach and eat ice cream!

LITTLE EMMETS: *(Ecstatic.)* Yes, yes yummy yummy!

LOWENNA: *(Nods.)* If you step on a weaver fish, just piss on your foot!

(Mrs Emmet hurries her family out the door. Exit Emmets stage right.)

LOWENNA: *(Giggles.)* What a tuss he is!

Sketch 6 - The beach, afternoon.
Emmet family standing together centre stage with coloured buckets and spades, Mr Emmet holding car keys.

MRS EMMET: Whitehouse beach is such a good place to spend the day. The paddling pool is ideal for the twins, don't you think so, darling?

MR EMMET: I'd like to call on Dawn!

MRS EMMET: Dawn? Are we acquainted?

MR EMMET: Dawn French my dear! I have it in mind to purchase a number of her autographed books.

MRS EMMET: Well darling, if you wish to call on her, do go ahead, but the children are all sandy and it would be totally unsuitable for them to accompany you!

MR EMMET: Quite so. I will go alone.

LITTLE EMMETS: We want to see the mouse! Where's the mouse?

MRS EMMET: What mouse? *(Agitated.)* Where? Where's the mouse?

LITTLE EMMET 1: Lowenna said there's a mouse!

MR EMMET: Lowenna talks rubbish. There's no mouse!

LITTLE EMMET 2: She said there's a mouse in the mouse hole.

MR EMMET: Now stop that! You're upsetting your mother!

LITTLE EMMETS: Mummy wants to see the mouse too!

MR EMMET: That's enough.

(Mr Emmet exits stage left.)

PEN: Mr Emmet strides across the car park, muttering to himself. He jumps into his black BMW, slams the door *(Slamming sound.)* and, oh dear me, he reverses straight into a bollard. *(Crash sound.)*

LITTLE EMMETS: Ha ha ha

MRS EMMET: *(Waving.)* Have a good time darling!

PEN: Clutching one little Emmet in each hand Mrs Emmet

wanders over the beach, while the children collect shells in their buckets, look for crabs and watch the boats out on the horizon.

LITTLE EMMETS: Mummy, it's been a lovely day!

Sketch 7 Garage, late afternoon.
Chairs arranged as in a car: 2 at front, 2 at back.
(Mr Emmet is standing waiting to be served.)
TRISTAN: *(Tristan enters stage left, wiping his oily hands on his apron.)* Wasson me cock?
MR EMMET: Pardon?
TRISTAN: Bent your rear end?
MR EMMET: *(Ignoring the question.)* I need this fixed right away.
TRISTAN: Dreckly Sir, dreckly! We'll try to pull the dent out but if there's still a crease we'll need a replacement.
MR EMMET: The cost is no object, it's the timescale that's vital.
TRISTAN: Ah, timescale. *(Teasing.)* I may have to go to a breaker's yard.
MR EMMET: It must be the exact shade and colour: metallic pearl black.
TRISTAN: Of course! Let's have a good look. *(He examines the damage.)* Giss on! Drain plunger 'll pop that out!
MR EMMET: Stupid place to put a bollard. Right in my way! *(He exits stage right.)*
TRISTAN: My head is reeling from this man,
His head is like an old tin can,
A tin can filled with effervescence,
Effervescent words of nonsense.

All nonsensical amusement
Brought to nought by his abusement.
Fix your tin can right away
Of-course sir, anything you say!
Emmets always will be so
Uz poor Cornish ought to know
Our place, until they leave uz be.
Then 'ome we'll roam for oggy tea.
(Tristan bows.) Goodbye Lord Emmet, Earl of Chelsea!!!

Sketch 8 The B& B garden, early evening.

Gate with house name stage centre.

Lowenna is watering her flowers

(Mr Emmet enters stage right and stands stands at the open gate looking puzzled.)

LOWENNA: Wasson shag? *(She puts her watering can down.)*

MR EMMET: I am not accustomed to being greeted in this manner. Kindly refrain.

LOWENNA: Teazy are we? Your little ones are wanting to see you. All excited about the knockers on yon carn!

LITTLE EMMET 1: *(Running in from stage left.)* Daddy, daddy, we're taking oggies with us tomorrow, Lowenna says...

LITTLE EMMET 2: *(Following in from stage left.)* And we're going to climb Brown Willy to find the knockers.

MR EMMET: *(Looking hard at Lowenna.)* I think that, sadly, holding a conversation with a Cornish man, or woman, is impossible. You people can't help it!

LOWENNA: Your children understand me perfectly.

MR EMMET: *(Slowly.)* But as soon as you start talking to me...it's ...unintelligible! *(He points at the house name.)* What exactly is that?

LOWENNA: *(Curtsies.)* Treth Krowji ...Seaside Cottage. Sir! Welcome.

(Mrs Emmet enters coming from the house stage left. She stands watching.)

(Mr Emmet comes through the gateway and turns to close it.)

LOWENNA: Leave it abroad. Looks welcoming and more friendly that way.

MR EMMET: *(He leaves the gate open.)* And where did you pick up all this odd language?

LOWENNA: My good father, bless his soul. Back along 'e were a huer, watching for signs of the pilchard shoals. Have ee had a stargazy pie yet?

MRS EMMET: We must sample some while we're here. Where's the best place?

MR EMMET: Don't ask her! She'll send us to some dead end in the middle of nowhere!

MRS EMMET: Oh darling, I just remembered we have a Lonely Planet tourist book for Cornwall in the beemer. We can have a look in there...and how was Dawn?

MR EMMET: *(Ignoring her question.)* Ah yes, it's in the leather folder under the rear seat entertainment system.

(Mrs Emmet doesn't move.)

PEN: There is a long silence as they stand in the pretty garden, the sun shining down on Mrs Emmet's burnt shoulders and feet.

LOWENNA: *(Smiling at Mrs Emmet.)* It's a wonderful place,

Cornwall. Would you mind making a few comments in the visitors book?

MRS EMMET: Of course! Where is it?

LOWENNA: In the kitchen. Just tick the boxes, all graded from one to three, easy! Seven categories; attitude, efficiency, welcome, cleanliness, staff, helpfulness, and food......

MR EMMET: That's preposterous! Signing your visitors book – it's the last straw. Don't be so absurd!

MRS EMMET: Why are you so worked up darling?

MR EMMET: It's...it's ludicrous. We should have stayed at... the Headland. An upper class mansion is eminently more suitable than this ...this Treth Krowji!

LOWENNA: And I have some Cornish sun cream you can use, the best.

MRS EMMET: I shall recommend Treth Krowji to the rest of the world!

MR EMMET: You will not do any such thing.

LOWENNA: *(She belches loudly.)* Pardon me, such a meal I had, at the Nare!

PEN: Oh dear Lowenna, you've done it now!

LOWENNA: *(With a chuckle.)* I hear on the news there's a storm coming in.

MRS EMMET: According to the Times newspaper there'll be torrential rain with severe flooding. Do you have any sandbags, Lowenna?

MR EMMET: *(Interrupting.)* And travel chaos. So, I've decided to return home. We shall head back straight away.

LOWENNA: *(Laughs to herself.)* Right on! Typical of ants! The rain makes them pack up and high-tail it. Back through the bottlenecks!

LITTLE EMMETS: But Daddy!

MR EMMET: Now shut up and glue those little eyes to your Nintendo till we hit home!

(Mrs Emmet runs to fetch their belongings and casts a despairing look at Lowenna.)

LITTLE EMMETS: But Daddy, Lowenna said ...

MR EMMET: And mind where you put those buckets and spades and sun cream. And no sand!

(The Emmets all scramble through the gate.)

LOWENNA: *(She blows a kiss to the twins.)* Those Emmets, they clog our beaches six weeks of every year! *(She smiles and her eyes sparkle.)* Now there's a thought makes me happy...*(Places her hands on her hips.)*

LITTLE EMMETS: Bye 'wenna, love you 'wenna.

LOWENNA: *(She laughs and walks to stage centre front.)* When their exhaust pipes disappear past that there clump o' one hundred and forty beech trees!

PEN: Is this Lowenna's moment of triumph? We will leave you pondering!

LOWENNA: Cookworthy Knapp, what marks our border at Lifton! *(She shuts her eyes.)* My 'coming home' trees; nothing like the Liffey landmark!

Little Bear

by T J Dockree

Ursa closed her eyes to savour the wind and listen to the air. Waves cracked on the cliffs below and seagulls squawked their indifference at each other. Nothing yet.

She smiled. This was her favourite moment. Sitting on top of the Huer Hut. Waiting.

The seagulls notched up their noise. Ursa leant forward, attentive to the hues and colours of the sea below. A dark shadow was moving slowly into the mouth of the bay. Ursa scrambled up, grabbing the two furze bushes resting on the roof beside her. She waved them high above her head, stretching herself as tall as she could to make sure Jem could see her.

Jem jumped up from his lookout rock and shouted 'Hevva! Hevva!' The men on the beach scrambled to their places around Nellie's hull. With a nod from old Tom, they heaved Nellie from her resting place into the cold slap of the waves.

Jem crouched at the tiller and guided them through the swell towards Black Cliff, watching Ursa's signals closely.

'She's driving us onto the rocks.' Kas growled, 'She's going to kill us.' He glared at the wives and sweethearts waiting on the shore. 'The sea doesn't like women. They shouldn't be here.' He stabbed his finger at Ursa's silhouette above them. 'And that one's a witch!' A few of the men looked around uneasily.

'She's going to kill us all, she's ...'

'By God, if someone doesn't shut him up, I will!' yelled Jem. The furze bushes dropped low.

'They've gone.' Jem sighed and turned the boat away from the cliffs.

'They were never there. She tricked you. She just wants to kill us.'

'No. Ursa always gets us the catch. You frightened them off with your superstitious squealing. You just cost us a month's pay.'

The boat fell silent.

'To shore!'

Jem looked at the sun. It was getting late. He took off his cap and bowed to Ursa to let her know her shift was over.

Ursa waved back then jumped down from the roof. Inside, she lay the furze bushes next to her father's old coat, ready for the morrow. Just as he had always done.

There'd be no money today, but she still had some left over from last month and Farmer Joseph had promised her a comb of honey to make Hevva cake.

Jem jumped out of Nellie and pulled Kas to one side.

'You're done here. You won't be fishing with us again.'

'That's fine by me. Your boat is cursed. You're all going to die.' Kas watched Ursa leave the hut, then spat on the sand and left.

'That fella is eaten up with hate, Jem,' old Tom said as he puffed slowly on his pipe. 'I heard they lock their womenfolk up where he comes from, when they go to sea. His boat got burnt 'cos he beat his wife to death after a no catch. But it was the brother that did the burning went to prison 'cos the policeman there beats his wife up too.'

'You could have told me that a bit sooner. Like before we let him on the boat?'

'Might just be gossip.' Old Tom shrugged. 'You know how folks are.'

'All the same, I don't like the way he looked at Ursa.' Jem started to tidy up some rope, then threw it into the boat. 'Can I borrow your cart?'

Ursa climbed the headland path, a deep sandy gully, worn by centuries of walking. At the top it forked inland, through the wood to Joseph's farm. Ursa picked up a stick and swished it as she walked beneath the ancient trees. A branch cracked somewhere above and the noise echoed down toward her. Fat squirrel? She giggled. Her dad had named the sounds that scared her so she wouldn't be afraid.

A twig snapped on the path behind her. Probably just someone from the village. She ran. Joseph would be wondering where she was.

The wood ended below a field of poppies, rising up like a huge red barrel wave over the hill. The stream was usually a lazy snake, but today it was frantic and fast, hurrying towards the sea. It must have rained inland. Ursa looked up. Dark swollen clouds were swallowing up the light and she could smell the oncoming storm.

Ursa jumped across, then climbed the poppy hill to the farm. When she arrived, she found her favourite honey hustler, crabby old Joseph, nursing a stung hand.

'There you are. I kept some combs back for you. Help yourself.' He grunted at the bucket at his feet.

Ursa pulled out a honeycomb and broke it into her hand. Golden liquid oozed out, which she gently smeared over his stings. She found a dock leaf and plastered it on top of the stings with another slab of honey.

'You know that's a shilling's worth you just wasted.' He frowned but kept his hand out.

Ursa gave him two shillings and picked up another honeycomb. She gave him a parting wave, then skipped away back to the poppy field.

Joseph looked at his hand. It was getting windy and dust and farm debris now clung to the honeycase. He felt sticky and grubby, yet curiously happy. 'You know, it does feel better,' he thought. An uncharacteristic smile found its way to his mouth.

He watched Ursa bob away down the field, painting poppies with the honey still dripping from her hand.

'No fish today, Jem?' Jem smiled politely at old Tom's daughter and edged away, getting the cart ready. 'When are you going to find someone to help you look after little Ursa?' Nell leant next to him but Jem walked to the other side. 'She needs a mum.' Jem helped old Tom climb into the cart. 'You need a wife.'

Jem felt the heat in his neck but ignored it. He faced her.

'I like you Nell, I do, but if you genuinely care about Ursa, you don't need to be married to me to be a mum to her. And I'll be the one who decides if I need a wife.'

Jem pulled himself up into the cart.

'Sorry Tom.'

'She needed to be told, boy. Shame though, I'd have liked you for a son.' Old Tom winked at Nell, then clicked the horse to move on.

'Seriously though, she's not wrong. I know you and her dad were best friends, but as she gets older people are going to talk.' Old Tom chuckled and slapped Jem's knee. 'I've a very generous dowry saved up. You could buy Nellie outright. And you're not getting any younger, boy.'

'You are a bad man!' Jem shook his head.

When they reached the road, Sergeant Cooper came running towards them, waving his arms. 'Jem! Where's Ursa?'

'Up at Joseph's. Why?'

'We need to find her. Seems the new chap was muttering about burning the Hevva witch.'

'Hop up Sergeant. We're on our way to the farm now.'

As Ursa crossed back over the stream, a man appeared from between the trees. She remembered him from the beach, how the sun had shone on his curly blonde hair.

Kas walked towards her with a torch in his hand. The flames roared as they consumed the oil drenched rag and flickered dramatically in the wind.

'Hello witch.' He waved the torch backwards and forwards in front of her face.

Ursa stepped back, averting her head as the wind blew the flame closer.

'Your kind burnt my boat, so I'm going to burn you.' Kas jabbed the torch at her and Ursa shielded herself with her arms.

'Witches are afraid of fire, aren't they?' He drew the torch back, for a final fatal plunge, but the wind switched sides and fire exploded across Kas's head, setting his hair alight in a blazing halo. He screamed, then fainted, suddenly silent except for the consuming flames.

Ursa dropped down, smothering out the fire with her hands, then wrapped his burns in honey. She cradled his head in her lap and rocked backwards and forwards. Memory erupted in a howl of pain, her first sound since her father died.

Farmer Joseph had run as fast as his old legs would let him when he saw Kas waving the torch at Ursa. When he got to her side, he laughed at the honey casing on Kas's head, then gasped at the pain of his effort on his lungs.

'The fire's out now, child. You need to let him go so we can get him some help.'

Jem stopped the cart by the honey buckets, scattered on the ground where Joseph had dropped them. He jumped down and searched the yard.

'Ursa! Ursa!'

He spun around in a panic.

'No. No. I should have followed her. I took too long.'

'Jem! She's down by the stream,' called the Sergeant.

Kas began to stir. Joseph grabbed Ursa and pulled her away. 'Aarghh!' Kas lit up with the memory of excruciating pain. 'You burned me. You made it burn me.'

Joseph raised his honeyed hand and pointed at Kas's head.

'She saved your life. Who put that honey on your head? Huh? Piskies?'

Kas became aware of the oozing on his scalp. He saw the Sergeant approaching and pointed at Ursa, yelling, 'She's a witch. She burned me.'

'No, you were trying to burn her. And if you go waving fire about on a windy night, you're the one going to get burnt,' Joseph snorted.

'Kas Taran, you're under arrest for attempted murder.' The sergeant opened up his irons.

'You should be arresting her, not me.'

'It might be okay to kill women and children where you come from, but here you get hun-,' Sergeant Cooper noticed Ursa watching anxiously, 'you go to prison.' He snapped the irons shut around Kas's wrists. 'And I know Ursa wouldn't burn anyone. Her dad died in a fire. She doesn't start fires. She puts them out.'

'Poor little bird.' Joseph's eyes were a little more watery than usual. 'We found you holding yer dad and crying, just like you was holding that bad boy over there.'

Jem ran over and knelt down in front of Ursa.

He leant forward and looked into her eyes, as green as the sea she loved so much, 'You did well, Little Bear. You are wiser and kinder than anyone I know.'

Ursa smiled tearfully and hugged him.

'And stickier! Ursa, why is there honey all over my jumper?'

After the Daccarien Accord

by John Evident

As anyone can now tell you, in this day and age of 2030, the planet Daccaria can be found in the constellation of Orion, orbiting the star Mintaka. The star on the right of Orion's belt.

The Daccarien decided to make themselves known to the people of Earth because the planet's atmosphere was in danger of being decimated from an energy ribbon. This ribbon was travelling towards us due to a collision in space between two stars in the Vega system. Our astronomers recorded the event and the whole world could see the result as a sparkling blue star in the night sky, but none of the experts noticed the energy wave moving in our direction.

The visitors saved the planet's atmosphere by surrounding the Earth with a fleet of their ships. They created a shield by charging our planet's ionosphere to deflect the wave in a spectacular light show that lasted for several hours. Although this was an amazing feat undertaken by the visitors, it's all the other things they have done since, that I've put in this report.

After the danger passed, and everyone had calmed down from the incredible light display, a global dawning of realization swept across the face of the world. A palpable feeling of uneasiness overwhelmed us, because we now knew we were no longer alone in the universe. All the nations' governments were on tenterhooks, waiting to see what was next. There was growing anticipation of meeting these visitors from across the vastness of space.

The world did not have to wait long. The Daccarien requested a meeting with representatives from all the countries of the world. The request was made by Mason Samuelson on every TV channel around the globe. A time and place were given to all governments. They were instructed to make arrangements so the whole world could come together, and to assist those countries that did not have a Navy, as the location they picked was the middle of the Atlantic Ocean.

The nations of Earth were given four weeks to get their act together. No nation wanted to be left out and this motivated the world to achieve the deadline and meet the Daccarien.

Four weeks later, the first week of 2023, an armada of ships, the like of which had not been seen in the memory of mankind, congregated in the middle of the Atlantic at the given coordinates, all ready and waiting for the day to start. The televised footage of this event has gone down in the annals of Earth's history.

In the video you can see all the decks of the aircraft carriers crowded with people, looking like a gathering from the Olympics, with each group holding their country's flag aloft. Most individuals are craning their necks skyward, looking for the first signs. Then there is the moment when someone calls out and points, then a ripple of a murmur from all 127 carrier decks as everyone can see a squadron of jets emerge from the cloud cover.

Then a hushed silence as a shadow of epic proportions blots out the sun and the Daccarien ship slowly makes its appearance. The craft the world now knows as the Voss was a three-mile wide, delta-shaped spaceship. It descended as gently as a feather to the space left for them in the middle of the armada.

Following this was the time for the smaller craft to float out from the top of the Voss. I'm using the words 'smaller craft' lightly because they were still bigger than anything flying on Earth. These craft floated silently to designated carriers. There is a famous image of the USS Ronald Reagan almost dwarfed by one of these smaller craft and the representatives of earth walking on board via a gangplank of immense proportions.

With all these events televised, we were shown the delegates being invited into an arena the size of Wembley stadium. Mason is in a blue jumpsuit, standing on stage, welcoming all the delegates on board, but the atmosphere is very negative, with raised voices and jeering, and you can see Mason trying to calm everyone down. Only no one is taking any notice. Then, from stage left, strides a giant of a man. This Daccarien, for he was clearly not human, stood nine foot tall with sky blue hair, golden skin and sparkling green eyes.

From the other side of the stage walks another Daccarien, but this time female, with flowing navy blue hair, deep golden skin and, again, sparkling green eyes. Both male and female Daccarien are wearing opalescent, deep yellow jumpsuits.

While the delegates are accepting what they are seeing, a noise comes from the back of the stage, from a massive door opening, and on walks a Dragon. Yes, that's right, I said Dragon. A walking, talking, breathing creature with greeny purple scaled skin that moved with the grace of a cat, albeit a cat that would give the largest of elephants an inferiority complex.

Finally, to top that, you see the camera swing around, just in time to see a Daccarien swoop over the heads of the delegates and land on stage. She's also in a yellow jumpsuit, but with wings of pale blue feathers. So, there is Mason, now standing in the company of two giants, a Dragon and an angel.

Just as the crowd start to raise their voices again, the Dragon stretches out his neck and his huge wings, opens his mouth, clicks his teeth and belches out a plume of yellow-green fire. He utters one word, 'Quiet!' All the delegates stand silently in shock, more from the fact the Dragon spoke English and the message was loud and clear.

Then you see Mason walk forward to talk to everyone and give the speech that everyone on Earth now knows off by heart.

'I know this is a lot to take in ... but the Daccarien are, what our scientists call, a type 3 civilization ... And do come in peace ... They are a philanthropic race that want to help the people of Earth. Each nation will be given their team to work with, and discuss what your individual needs are ... but let me make one thing clear. Do not ask or expect any advanced weaponry; as I have said the Daccarien are a peaceful race and will not allow one nation to become superior over another ...'

All the things that transpired after these Accords, with our new friends from across the galaxy, clearly demonstrated that they wanted to help Earth on the path to becoming a type 1 civilization.

Now, after eight years, the Daccarien have ended hunger throughout this planet by placing their food and drinks dispensing technology in every city, town, village, and township. They are used by anyone who needs them, rich or poor.

Children no longer suffer from hunger, blindness or illness; Oxfam and the other charities have new helpers from across the galaxy.

They have purified the pollution in our planet's groundwater, rivers and streams, including taking all the plastics from our oceans. The beaches of Cornwall and the rest of the world are finally clear.

They've added their technology to all the water treatment plants around the world. Their filtration systems clean the wastewater far beyond anything that had been achieved by man, making the discharge back into the ocean the best it's ever been. I know the surfers around Cornwall are happy about it.

One of their bigger gifts to the world was their cloning technology. Back in 2023 millions of individuals who, through no fault of their own, found themselves paraplegic or quadriplegic, were given the gift of having their consciousness placed in a Daccarien clone. They now work as part of the crew on board their ships.

It was learnt that all Daccarien can have a new body, if they feel their old one is wearing out, but you're still talking of 250 years on average per cloned body. This offer has now been given to any individual on Earth who wishes to truly live forever and see the wonders of the Daccarien Galactic Federation for themselves. As you can imagine, the people of Earth have really got behind that one.

The other really big change is no one dies from cancer anymore. The Daccarien have guided our scientists and doctors to eradicate 99% of Earth's disease and ailments. The common cold and flu have finally been given the boot. Daccarien medicines are so far advanced, they seem like magic.

I can remember waking up one morning, in my flat in Newquay. My girlfriend was all excited telling me that, on the news, the Daccarien had tackled climate change in our atmosphere and the air we breathe. Using their molecular technology, they've not only reduced carbon dioxide and the other greenhouse gasses, but they've also increased oxygen levels.

The human race had become so adapted to the slow build-up of toxins in our water table and atmosphere, that, to breathe the richness of this clean stuff in for the first time, was pure bliss. Not unlike when they cleaned the water of all the pollution around the world. To drink from a simple tap was suddenly like drinking the purest spring water.

They have even fixed the hole in the ozone layer and purified the land around Chernobyl, (that area in the Ukraine that's been a no-go since 1986). All to show their willingness to help the Accords along!

I leave this writing a moment to get a drink.

You know, personally, I think they chose the right guy to invite on board their ship and become their ambassador, because, if it had been me, I don't think things would have worked out the same way. My friend Mason, the delivery driver, was the type of guy always on hand to help anyone who needed it. Nothing was ever too much bother. He would go out of his way to make sure the job was finished on time. I can imagine him seeing it as a challenge, bringing the whole world together and solving all their problems. Even if the troublemakers of this world do accuse Mason of being a traitor and selling out his planet!

Ok back to the report...

Those magical actions and changes have won over the people of this globe. To experience true kindness and a caring nature from a race of beings, genuinely happy to help improve a planet's health and well-being, simply because they can, is a powerful emotion.

As a part of the continuation of the accords, the Daccarien made changes to the infrastructure of everyday life, to move the world along to becoming a type 1 civilization, to make energy available to everyone.

One day, all homes in Cornwall woke up to find alien technology, in the form of a small white box covering their electric meters and a sensor, on every roof of every home, shop and industrial unit. Through the media, the Daccarien informed residences in Cornwall they no longer needed to pay for electricity. It was now free to use.

With all buildings and places now having Daccarien technology, we simply draw electricity straight from the ionosphere, very much like Nikola Tesla wished to do many years ago.

The Daccarien also added their technology to rigs in the North Sea, extracting the gas and refining it, then sending it directly to the homes of Cornwall, making it free to use. As you can imagine, since this technology has gone global, there are a lot of people, including myself and my family, who feel very happy with not having to pay energy bills anymore.

But there was still a lot of negative feeling surrounding this change. The loudest came from the now-defunct energy companies around the globe that were no longer needed, all stating the same thing: 'The Daccarien didn't ask, they just went ahead and did it.'

This build-up of anger was shared by all the world's military. Even after the speech by Mason at the Accords, most nations still brought up the topic of advanced weapons, but the Daccarien wouldn't have any of it.

This frustration finally reached boiling point in 2026, when one nation launched a nuclear missile at a Daccarien ship. Nothing happened to the craft. Their molecular defence system simply disintegrated the missile into dust, but the nations of the world collectively held their breath to see what our new friends from across the galaxy would do in response.

Nothing prepared Earth for what they did next.

It turned out that the Dragons are the ruling class in Daccarien society. They were not happy that a species as young as ours were ready to use such weapons. So, they decided to take the toys off the children. Within the hour, all the ships that were still orbiting the planet synchronized their molecular weapons and sent a beam over the surface of the Earth. The people of Earth knew something had changed, because the skies glowed brightly for a few seconds, but it was not obvious what had happened at first.

Then, slowly, reports started coming in to news channels that conflicts around the world had stopped, stating that all weapons, like guns, tanks, mines, knives and hand grenades, had turned to wood. The nuclear nations rushed to their silos to find that their ICBMs were still in place but were now made of polished teak. Even the captains, on board nuclear submarines under the ocean, stood baffled at seeing a row of gleaming lumps of wood where once stood trident missiles.

My thoughts at the time had been: World peace in one fell swoop!

The public census worldwide was positive to this move by the Daccarien, because we no longer had mutual nuclear destruction hanging over us.

And yet, as with all things the Daccarien did, there were exceptions. Law enforcement agencies around the world now sport new, advanced, non-lethal, stun weaponry, to help them keep the peace when doing their daily duties.

Planes can still fly, including military jets, but the jets can't shoot at each other unless they use bows and arrows or throw rocks at one another.

So, these are just some of the things that have

happened to our world since the Daccarien have arrived and there is no putting the genie back in the bottle. They really would be missed if they went.

Well, as a favour to a friend of the ambassador, myself and my family have been invited to live on board, like Mason. So, I'm off to have my consciousness put into one of those cloned bodies and see all the wonders of the Galactic Federation for myself, as part of the crew. A bit of a step up from driving a van around Cornwall.

Hang on a moment. A thought just occurred to me and I need to see Mason about this.

If a race of advanced beings, who did not believe in taking lives, decided to conquer a planet, what better way than create a problem in space with their advanced technology and turn up on the planet that's in grave danger with all the answers. Then gradually, with their cloning technology, turn the inhabitants of the world into Daccarien.

Yet everyone is happier than they have ever been. Even the people in the energy industry have been given new jobs on board Daccarien spaceships, working in the engineering bays. They are now learning about how zero-point energy makes the ships move. And all the Earth's military personnel now work as part of the Daccarien First Contact Pathfinder Squads in their new cloned bodies.

And with the help of our new friends, NASA, ESA, The Russian Space Agency, Japan, China and India now have a base on the Moon and one on Mars, each in the form of an older Daccarien ship no longer used in the fleet; with all the nations on board working together. There's a great feeling all round!

I can't do justice with the right expressive words to get across to you the sensation of heightened exuberant awareness. It's like a kind of aliveness that has affected the deepest level of your inner consciousness, a different way of thinking. The sheer knowingness that has touched everyone's soul on Earth; that things are better than before, a lush, living, warming comfort coming from an advanced higher intelligence that is ready to help.

It's like the whole world has changed. There's a heartfelt joy at the way we look at the planet now. Everyone is more relaxed because a global crisis will no longer trouble this protected planet. A new, vivid reality that says there's more good to come and things are simply going to get better.

Finally, to close this report, a strange fact you might like to know. To help Dragons fly and get their huge bulk off the ground, they need to eat large quantities of raw meat so they can metabolize the protein into a natural form of hydrogen. This hydrogen is held in bladder type organs that run along the inside of their bodies on either side of their spine. To descend, they expel the surplus gas they don't need by clicking their back teeth that are very close to a kind of flint-like substance; thus igniting it into flames.

But I wonder what kind of raw meat?

Nixie's Quest

by Angela Evron

Nixie struggled to swim as ten-foot waves reached a crescendo. She needed to get to Chapel Rock, and fast. There was not much time before the tide receded. A rip current caught her, and she tumbled round and round, twisting like a tornado. Summoning her strength, she pushed through onto the crest of the wave, instead of finding safety beneath it.

She glanced across, checking for surfers; she could not risk being seen. There were only two, far in the distance – too far to notice her.

She could hear her father now, his booming voice reprimanding her. 'Nixie! Have you ventured into forbidden territory again?' She was glad his voice was only in her head.

Nixie pushed him from her mind and concentrated on reaching the rock before the storm, but the tidal force was like a vacuum pulling her under into the deep water below. She focused her mind.

'I can do this,' she chanted, flapping harder with a strength she hadn't realised she possessed. Meeting the crest of the wave, she jumped its height and rode it to the tip of the rock, pulling herself onto land.

Nixie scanned the area; she was safe. Taking a deep breath, she inhaled land oxygen into her lungs, relishing the sensation. Across the beach, the tide almost spilt over the sea wall. The oncoming storm would wash their land-filth into the ocean.

Nixie sighed.

Once her eyes adjusted, she fixed her gaze along the edge of the golden sand to the new development of luxury beach apartments. The builders were working, despite the impending weather. Anger surged through her like a toxin and she despised the feeling.

'I'll find a way,' she said. 'I won't let you get away with this.'

She heard the Air Sea rescue helicopter hovering in the distance. Without haste, she slid from the rock safely back into the ocean.

Tomorrow, she would meet Asrai at the caves.

The morning's low tide had Nixie scanning for microplastics on the seabed. Some would not be visible to a human eye, but Nixie's eyes could magnify the sea creatures, who were sucking up the plastics as food. She observed them with a heavy heart.

Flapping her tail to swim up, a sound wave coming from the pod changed her track. As she surfaced, she expected to see Beau among the dolphins, jumping above the waves. But he wasn't there – and they weren't playing. They seemed troubled.

Where was Beau?

As she glided through the water towards them, she heard a cry. It was him!

Following the sound, she found him trapped in a fishing net. He flapped slowly, losing energy.

'Don't panic, Beau!' She dived beneath him, trapping her own tail in the mesh, but managing to free herself again. She grabbed a sharp piece of coral, severed the knotted strands, and untangled the net.

Beau let out a grateful trill as he swam free.

'Quick, before they know you've been near the shore! They'll separate us if we're caught again!'

Beau flipped her onto his back and she gripped his dorsal fin as he sped off.

She slid off his back once they neared his pod. He tapped her playfully with his nose and she laughed before swimming away.

Making her way towards the caves, she manoeuvred around the rocks until safely hidden from the clifftop. She eased herself up onto a flat rock, allowing the waves to bathe her as she plaited her golden hair. Her emerald tail glistened brightly against the gunmetal rock, turning different shades as the water ebbed and flowed.

'Have you seen the beach?'

Nixie flinched. 'I wish you wouldn't creep up on me like that, Asrai!'

'Fairies don't creep. They hover.'

'Well, at least hover in my peripheral vision. Why are

you up there? You're supposed to be an aquatic fairy. You spend more time on land!'

'And you're a mermaid, and so do you! Sorry if I made you jump.'

Nixie chuckled. 'You were saying?'

'Nothing changes – in fact, it's worse than ever. The usual picnic rubbish being dumped. There's new stuff every day.' Asrai glided down to the rock, pulled in her small translucent wings and sat shading her fragile body from the direct sunlight.

'I know. It's bad enough leaving soiled nappies, but now they're in plastic sacks too,' said Nixie despondently. 'All their human waste as well as everything else!' She sighed. 'What about the building site?'

'More water bottles and sandwich wrappers. They just toss them over the wall. As if we haven't enough problems with the tourists.'

'I'm beginning to despise humans.'

'They're not all bad,' said Asrai. 'The landlady at the beach bar does a regular beach clean with the locals. You should see the amount they collected this morning after the tide went out!'

'Beau got stuck in a net just now. Even the net had plastic wedged between the holes.'

Asrai gasped. 'Is he hurt?'

'Not this time. He was shaken up, though, and—' There was a low rumble beneath the waves. 'Oh no! That will be Father. I must go, quick!' Nixie slid to the base of the rock.

'Wait! What shall I tell Wiggy?'

'To find out when the human's taking his boat out.'

'Let's meet here at the same time tomorrow, tide pending.'

Nixie inched into the water. 'Or high tide later if you have news. I'll try to get back.'

Asrai flapped above her, hovering like a sparrowhawk, then flew towards the shore and out of sight.

Nixie had to execute her plan, and soon. So far, she'd learned the developer's name was Rupert – stupid name, she thought – and, thanks to Wiggy's brilliant earwigging, she'd learned of other plans. It was useful having a pixie as her land spy. Asrai and Wiggy made a good team and Nixie felt blessed to have such good friends.

Rupert, she'd discovered, intended to build more houses around the coastline, aside from the luxury beach-side apartments. That meant even more waste.

At high tide, the raging storm meant that Asrai wouldn't be at the rock, but Nixie pushed down her disappointment at having to wait another day. In the depths of the ocean, she joined her family. She heard Syrena practising her song.

'Does that song lure all fishermen?'

'What are you up to?'

'Nothing.'

'I can hear those curious cogs turning in that brain of yours. Have you been up there taking risks again?' Syrena flipped her raven hair and fixed wide aqua eyes on her cousin, waiting.

'I only want to make things right.'

'This fixation of yours will get you into deep water, if you'll pardon the pun. You'll never keep the ocean free of pollution. It won't work.'

'They're destroying our planet! Won't you help me, please?'

'And have the wrath of your father's tongue? Oh no, not me! And you ... you must keep away from land, Nixie. You risk getting us seen, and that would be disastrous. I won't tell Zorca this time, but this is your last warning. Do you understand?'

'Yes,' she said, floating away. It was clear she would need more cunning and caution. Even Syrena – who could lure the most experienced of fishermen to their deaths – was not on her side.

The storm lifted the following morning, and the ocean was fresh with renewed oxygen.

After a feast of seaweed, Nixie was allowed her daily freedom.

She frolicked through the distant waves, playing with Beau, thinking up a plan. She would have to find a way to get Rupert under the ocean. Dare she visit the sea witch for a metamorphosis potion? Nixie shuddered at the thought, and dismissed that option.

Bidding Beau farewell, she sped to the cave to meet Asrai.

'Wiggy says he's taking the boat out at the weekend, once the stormy weather has settled.'

'Have you flown around the site?'

'Yes. I saw them again. They stayed late last night, tossing glass beer bottles over the wall. Wiggy told me they even had the cheek to play a game earlier in the day.'

'What game?'

'Whose water bottle would be first to catch a wave and

disappear!' Asrai's wings flapped rapidly, her delicate aqua-blue body shaking with anger. 'But Wiggy's been busy. He rounded up the pixies to join forces and help him.' Asrai smiled. 'They've been hiding the builders' tools at night.' She chuckled. 'They think the site is haunted.'

Nixie laughed. It felt so good to laugh for a change, instead of feeling annoyed.

'Good for Wiggy. Ask him to keep his special ears open to find out about times.'

'Will do.'

Sunset was Nixie's favourite time. As the sun cast its golden glow, a sea of stars twinkled, lighting up the ocean. It was a spectacular sight. The ocean was still – the calm after the storm, and the waves not favourable for surfers. The bathers had gone, too; the spring day meant cold water once the sun went down.

The day's few tourists had retreated to their city lives, leaving only the locals who knew and respected the sea, unlike the visitors who thought they could defy nature's elements. Some humans were stupid, braving the sea even when warned not to. They refused to consider riptides and, as a result, some drowned. Others got drunk at the beach bar and skinny-dipped at night; they were usually too paralytic to notice Nixie and Beau pushing them safely to shore.

Nixie swam to the craggy rocks and could hardly believe her luck. He was there, on a small boat, casting a fishing line – alone.

Swimming up closer, she watched him for a while. He grabbed a bottle of beer, tipped the contents down his throat and tossed the bottle into the sea.

It incensed her. Ducking under the water, she motioned to Beau to join her.

'Now. But just a nudge.'

Beau circled the boat, and it rocked. Rupert looked around, then stood up.

'Now that's stupid.' Nixie shook her head, smiling as he tried to keep his balance.

Beau leapt out of the water, only metres away. Startled, Rupert lost his balance and toppled overboard. Nixie raced to the boat and plunged beneath. He was thrashing around, his head bobbing up and down.

He couldn't swim!

She darted behind him and pushed him up. He scrambled to safety, coughing and spluttering.

He peered over the bow just as she popped her head above the water.

'Not a great swimmer, are you?'

'Where did you come from?'

'I swim around these rocks often. I saw you fall in.'

'Well, you must be a good swimmer, out at this distance.' He shook the water from his hair and dug his thumbs into his ears.

She smiled, being careful to keep her powerful tail hidden. 'I practise daily.'

'Want to come aboard?'

'With you? No thanks.'

'Why not? I've got beer.'

'I saw. I've been watching you. I don't like what I see.'

'Watching me?'

'Yes, tossing your rubbish overboard. It's disgusting!'

'So what? It's only a bottle – I'm sure this ocean is vast enough to swallow it.'

'You have no respect for the planet, do you?'

'What's your problem? You don't even know me.'

Nixie stared at him. 'That's where you're wrong. I know you're some big-time developer, eating up the coastline with your holiday homes, swamping the green belt. I've seen you down there' – she nodded towards the shore – 'working on those apartments.'

'What gives you the right to judge me?'

'I have every right. Your builders dump their bottles over the wall every day. Do you have any idea how much rubbish damages our seas?'

He put his hands on his hips. 'No, but I'll bet you're going to tell me.'

'Millions of tonnes every year. Doesn't that concern you?'

'Nope. Why should it?'

'For a start, it's ingested by all species of the marine world.'

'So?'

'Are you stupid?' Nixie's lungs heaved. 'Those bits of plastic are entering the food chain ... your food chain!'

He laughed. 'Not mine, I hate fish.'

'I can't believe I just saved your life. Next time you won't be so lucky.'

'Thanks. Now go away and leave me in peace.'

Nixie was so incensed by his rudeness that she rocked the boat.

'You're crazy! You won't shake me off!' he shouted, gripping tight to the side.

Nixie whistled. Beau nudged the boat once more.

'Aarrgh!'

Splash!

Nixie swam to his side. His eyes were wide with shock and he fought against the water, sinking. She placed a conch over his nose.

'Breathe – and stop panicking.' She pulled him onto her back, pulling his arms around her neck. She swam deeper, passing a multitude of marine life. Rupert kicked her back, trying to free himself.

'Stop struggling or you'll die!'

Deep in the seabed, in her private kingdom, Nixie set him down and secured him to a bed of coral.

'Mer ... mermaids aren't real,' he blurted, after removing the conch. Instantly, he gasped for breath. Bubbles rose from his mouth.

'Keep that over your face. It allows you to exist for a while down here.'

'Why am I seeing an ocean nymph? I'm dreaming. No, wait – I'm dead, aren't I?'

'You soon will be if you keep removing that shell. Now, listen – this is our domain and I'm going to show you how you're destroying it.' Nixie twisted seaweed around his body with magical speed, leaving his arms free, and secured the other end to her waist. 'Prepare yourself for a journey of discovery.'

Nixie glided around the ocean floor, pausing to show Rupert the volume of debris. Avoiding her own home, she then took him to the surface, allowing him some air.

She swam among the floating debris for a while, then returned to the depths of the ocean. Her last stop was beneath the cliff where a crate was jammed into a sea rock. Trapped inside it was a dead mermaid, her body covered in holes where marine life had feasted. Rupert's head jolted back as Nixie purposely positioned his face next to the mermaid's dead, staring eyes. Her hair floated through the holes in the crate and brushed against his face. He batted it away in terror.

'This was my sister, Lorelei. She's fish food now, instead of turning to sea foam as we do when our natural timespan comes to an end.' Anger and grief fuelling her, she pulled him like a tugboat to the surface.

Back at his boat, she heaved him on board and set him free. He removed the shell, gasping for air.

'I'm alive! I'm not dreaming, or dead! What the hell just happened?'

'I showed you the error of your ways. You'll have no memory of what happened, only a tiny seed in your subconscious, like a dream. After all, mermaids aren't real, are they?'

'Nobody would believe me, anyway. I drink too much. But I don't understand – why didn't I die from lack of oxygen?'

'Our ocean feeds the earth most of its oxygen. You destroy it, you die. Respect it! The conch you wore has magic properties ... now I've used it, I've lost a hundred years off my lifespan, but it was worth it.'

He bowed his head. 'I'm sorry.'

'Then do something about it.'

Rupert sat back on his knees, pondering. 'I have to build. People need homes and whatever you think of me, I create jobs.'

'And pollution.'

He scratched his head. 'I could donate our profits to research. Maybe reusing plastic and never disposing of it?'

'You need to do more. Building in coastal regions puts more pressure on our marine ecosystems. And ... this will be your kingdom, too.'

'What do you mean?'

'Some humans think they have an afterlife. Do you?'

'I'd like to think there's something up there, yes.'

'Well, you're all wrong – and if you don't stop, we're all doomed. You think your souls are immortal, but you only live three hundred years, like us. That's what we have. This is where you end up. There are no heavenly spirits, only water spirits.'

'You're wrong!'

'You will become a merman once your earthly vessel decays. Half fish, half human.'

'I don't believe you.'

A clap of thunder made Rupert jump. Nixie looked up at the sky.

'When the lightning comes, look at the water. I'm allowing you one more piece of magic: a look into your future. I've spared you this time, because you've got a job to do.'

Nixie counted.

When the sky lit a bright white sheet, Rupert stared at the sea. He recoiled.

Nixie grinned. 'Do you like your blue tail? You have to earn a green one.'

He was stunned into silence.

Another jagged fork of lightning brought another

image: Rupert trapped inside a fishing net full of plastic debris, clawing his hands through the holes and flapping his tail for freedom.

'No!' he cried.

'This is the afterlife – your afterlife, and all the other humans.' If you don't clean up your act, it will destroy the planet. The fate of us all is in your hands. You still have a choice – for now at least.' Nixie turned to swim away.

'Wait! What's your name?'

'Nixie.'

'Will I see you again?'

'Not prematurely, I hope, but that's up to you.'

Knights On A Train

by T J Dockree

The buffet car yanked around a bend in the track. Sonja kept her hood up and her head down and took a deep breath. She'd got this far. The worst was over. She wasn't going to start flaking out now. Not when she was so close to freedom.

She hunted for an empty seat and found one by the window. Hedges and trees next to the track zipped past at speed, followed more sedately by those huddled together on sloping fields, offering cover to the cattle sheltering from the rain.

The warm ridges of the cardboard coffee cup felt comforting to her hands. Sonja sipped her latte and started to relax. She'd never got this far before. Was she dreaming? She leant back in the seat and exhaustion claimed her.

When she awoke, the world outside her window was dark. Her reflection peered at her, like some ghost, with chopped hair, owlish brown eyes and sunlight starved skin. She became aware of travelling companions at her table. She turned and a gleaming helmet, visor down, gently nodded at her. His startling white tunic was emblazoned with a crimson cross. Two more knights nodded at her then looked away.

'Tickets, please!' the ticket inspector called as he entered the carriage.

The knights already held theirs in shiny, spiked gauntlets. Shiny, except for the knuckles, which looked well used.

Sonja grabbed her bag and motioned to the knight next to her that she wanted to get out. He appeared not to notice.

'Excuse me, can you let me out, please?'

There was no response.

'Excuse me ....'

'Tickets! Hello gentlemen. Love the outfits!' The ticket inspector held his hand out for their tickets, but the knights didn't move. He frowned, then plucked the ticket from the gauntlet of the nearest knight.

'Mm. Falmouth. Ah, off to the jousting at Pendennis Castle then?' enquired the inspector with a chuckle. He proffered the ticket back. The knight remained motionless. The inspector frowned again and waved the ticket in front of his visor.

'Wow! Mannikins! That is so cool! And a ticket each too.' He looked across at Sonja. 'Are you an artist? You know it would have been cheaper to put them on the postal train? But I can see why you'd want them with you. They're fantastic!' He stepped back and looked under the table.

'Boots and all! That is amazing!' He inserted the ticket back into the knight's gauntlet and checked the other two.

'All in order. Just need your ticket now, ma'am.'

Sonja passed her ticket to him. She thought about explaining but felt too awkward. She smiled shyly instead.

Once the inspector had gone, she hid her face from the knights with her hand and looked outside. The sky was clear, a light grey framing a silhouette of hills and trees. A shaft of moonlight streaked towards her, highlighting everything in its path with a silvery white glow, like a fluorescent negative. She'd not seen moonlight do that before.

After a while she opened her fingers up slightly to sneak a peek at her trio of bodyguards. Why were they all looking at her earlier? Were they from Melzidek?

Or were they robots? Was someone operating them? Sonja studied the window to find the reflection of the people across the gangway at the opposite table. A young mum was sitting there, with a toddler standing on her lap, his face pressed against their window.

The train was slowing down. Sonja looked for a station name sign. The train clanked to a standstill, but she couldn't see a platform.

Someone outside shone a torch at her window. She shrank down. Did they see her?

Fists started banging on the side of the train.

'Open up! We have you surrounded and if you do not open up, we will shoot at you!'

The child at the other table grabbed at his mum and started to cry. His mother hugged him and held his head into her shoulder, away from the noise.

161

Sonja closed her eyes. *They've found me. Did I really think I could get away? They always find me. And I've put these people in danger.*

The ticket inspector ran to one of the doors.

'Hey guys! What's this all about? How can I help you?'

There was silence, then Sonja heard the voice that had first called to her five years ago.

'Open up! You have a girl on board who belongs to me. Let me have her and the rest of you will go free!'

'The doors have safety locks. They won't open unless we're at a station.'

'You're lying. You're trying to buy yourself some time until the police get here. Open up! Or we will shoot at the train.'

'Woah, steady on! I'll see if I can get the doors unlocked for you! Just give me a minute!'

'One minute is all you have ... 1 ... 2 ...'

The ticket inspector grabbed his radio.

'Buddy! How close are you? I can't stall them any longer!'

'... 11 ... 12 ... 13 ...'

'Buddy! Are you there?'

'... 21 ... 22 ...'

A disembodied voice crackled above them.

'Good evening ladies and gentlemen. We are currently experiencing a slight hold up. Please remain where you are. All our windows have toughened glass, but we do recommend you adopt the brace position for safety. Lean forward, so that you are away from the windows, and protect your head with your hands or a coat or a bag.'

'... 59 ... 60 ... Fire!'

Bullets hammered at the door and windows. The glass above Sonja split into frozen particles and started to sag.

Sonja slid under the table, finding a small space that wasn't filled with chainmail legs. She wondered if chainmail was bulletproof.

Between the legs and across the aisle she could see two pairs of eyes blinking back at her. The mother and son opposite had followed the same survival instinct.

Bullets clanged and popped against the wall of the train, next to her. The safety glass above was torn away and a shower of glass granules fell onto the table, spraying itself onto the seats and floor, wherever an opening could be found. The boy opposite cried loudly.

A smoking cannister landed in the gangway but an armoured hand picked it up and lobbed it back outside.

Something thudded below the window just above Sonja's head. She moved away and six chainmail legs tried to stand, drawing their swords.

'They've got guns! Guns beat swords!' Sonja hissed at them, 'And how did you manage to get swords on board a train?'

Above her she heard a scream as an unsuspecting face came violently into contact with a spiked gauntlet.

A blue light strobed into the carriage and lit up the seat next to her. A short blip of siren sounded out.

'Put your weapons down! We have you surrounded!'

Bodies banged against metal next to Sonja. She backed away into a metal leg.

'Is everyone okay in there?' a voice shouted up to them.

'Buddy! What took you so long, brother? I thought

we'd have to do your job for you!'

'Sam! How are you doing? Have you got any casualties? The paramedics are on their way down.'

'I'll do a check. Is it safe to come out from under the tables yet?'

'We've got all of them. The guy with the red tattoo across his face sends his regards!'

The ticket inspector unlocked the train door. A couple of men in bottle green uniform scrambled up followed by a concerned, wiry policeman.

'Good to see you, Sam. We need to chat to your passengers. We're hoping some of them might have more information for us about this Melzidek and what he's up to.'

'I don't suppose you've got any spare cars to take some of these folks home. This train isn't going anywhere until these windows are fixed.'

'They're kind of full of bad guys, but I'm sure they'd make room for you!' Buddy laughed.

Sam squatted down to look for Sonja. He found her looking up at him. He smiled and reached his hand out to her.

'You're safe now. You can come out,' he called to her gently.

Chainmail legs shuffled back to give her room to move. Sonja crawled out and took his hand. He helped her to her feet, then ducked down again to help mother and child back to their seats.

'It might be a little less draughty at their table.' Sam ushered Sonja onto a seat, winked at the boy and picked up his radio. 'Driver! Good work up there! We've got a few broken windows down here. What's the procedure?'

Sam and Buddy walked through the carriage, inspecting the damage, leaving them with two policemen. One of them offered his hat to the boy to play with.

'Good evening ladies and gentlemen. Thank you for being so calm and brave and so very patient during this attack on our train. Carriages with broken windows will now be closed. Will all passengers please move to carriages between the buffet car and the front of the train so that we can continue our journey and get you safely home. All passengers will be provided with tokens for free refreshments from the buffet car.'

Sonja stayed with the mother and child for the rest of the journey. The last she saw of the knights they were looking ahead, guarding the window, just as when she'd first seen them.

Sonja visited Falmouth a few months later to watch the jousting at Pendennis Castle. A trio of crusader knights, wearing white tunics with a crimson cross, stood guard outside the gatehouse.

As she passed, she caught herself staring at them. Did that knight just wink at her?

By Any Other Name

by Joshua Copus-Oxland

The piskie scouted the faraway island from her branched perch on the coast of Marazion. Water sloshed at the banks of the shore. Birds her size sang nearby. This would've been a peaceful scene if not for the large head poking out of the island's stone fort like a mole over a burrow. The owner of this head was the maligned giant Cormoran. After a ruckus caused by the humans and the mediators of her piskie village, they decided someone had to resolve this gargantuan issue. This piskie volunteered, curious, but undeterred in the face of danger. So, she beat her wings and sprang off the tree branch, journeying over to the anomaly in the middle of the ocean.

The piskie hid herself well, taking cover behind one of the fort's many white granite stones. Unaware of the interloper's presence, the giant stared at a cow cupped in one palm, his other hand brushing away long strands of hair as they swayed in the breeze. His eyes were hungry, yes, but displayed no malice in that soft, round face. Still, she had a job to do. As disgusting as it sounded, she followed the village elder's lead: to fly into the giant's ear and shout into it. So, she did, spelunking its waxy insides. Bleh. So much for her leaf clothes. A good telling-off was in order.

'Oi!' she shrieked, 'What do you think you're doing, stealin' their cattle? You oughta be ashamed of yourself!'

'Why is it any of your business?' the giant's deep voice echoed, loud enough that it vibrated inside the ear.

'Well, the humans were complainin', so of course it's my beeswax! Speaking of wax...' She trailed off in disgust.

'Were you forced to come here, then?'

'Yes. No. Probably would've come anyway.'

There was a pause. 'You are a brave soul. Can you come out?'

'For you to do what, exactly? Crush me in your hands and grind me into a powder to use for, er, whatever it is you do?'

'Of course not. I wish no harm upon your kind. It is just courteous, that is all.'

The piskie took a deep breath. She couldn't believe she was doing this, but she emerged to fly in front of his broad face, pouting at him. Her heart beat like the bard's leather drum, but she wouldn't show it, lest the giant see her weakness and bite her head off then and there.

'What is your name?' he asked.

She stopped to consider.

'Er, I dunno. We don't get given names. Everyone knows us anyway.'

'Why?'

'Not much point. It's not like them animals down there get names; not that it matters, since you're eatin' them either way. You'd probably do the same to me.' The giant frowned. 'Not true.' He gestured to the struggling livestock in his meaty paw. 'These animals cannot gain their own identity and do not have the right to a name. I have no remorse eating them, and must do so to preserve my kind.' He patted his thin belly. 'I am careful not to eat more than necessary.'

The piskie winced. 'Well, that makes sense, but...'

'But you are intelligent. I would never eat another being who could gain an identity of their own like yourself. So, if you do not have a name, let me think of one myself. My name is Cormoran, for instance.'

'Right...' The piskie turned, about to fly off. This talk wasn't as exciting as she hoped, not to mention too verbose for her liking, but at least the giant seemed harmless. Relatively speaking.

'Wait,' Cormoran called, soft enough that it didn't ring through the air, but loud enough for his word to carry weight. 'Will I see you again?'

The piskie turned, puzzled. 'No need to. I'll just tell my kind to make do with what they have, and if they don't like it, that's their problem.'

'So, will you not stop me?'

'Eh, if they complain some more, maybe I will.'

'Then ...' he grinned, 'that means I will have to cause more trouble.'

She tilted her head before flying off towards the mainland.

Seconds, minutes, and perhaps hours dragged on for the piskie as she foraged through the woods with her fellow fairy folk. Though the raspberries they picked were almost as large as they were, they carried them in many numbers, transporting them to the nearest human village to gain provisions for their own land, from old books to discarded music instruments. Foraging was second nature to her, as well as dodging the familiar dangers such as spider webs and bird habitats. That was all she was: a forager. And as far as the rest of the piskies were concerned, they seemed content in their daily routine.

Once the shift was over, the nameless piskie sat atop a tree branch and stared at Abmeth Gwig, a village of her kind which sat atop the barrows of Kernow, unsullied by human feet. Of course, there were a few piskies that liaised with the humans, but aside from that, the land went untouched.

It was such a tiny world down there. While she was satisfied with her upbringing to an extent, not expecting much else except for dancing with the merry piskies in the downtime, she yearned for something bigger. She had no possessions, not even a name, but the giant Cormoran had an island to himself. He wouldn't have posed a threat to them, and yet they wrote myths and songs about him and his terrible presence. Even his name took on different forms there. The commune was her identity while the giant had his own. Why didn't she? Perhaps she was just another grape in the fermenting barrel.

The previous talk kept her gears spinning, however. She thought of possible names for the villagers. There was the bard who she imagined as Borsed. There was the talkative piskie, who she imagined as Wedhel because of all her gossiping. And finally, there was the teacher, who she imagined as Tardra because he always drove her to sleep in their lessons.

Before she could think on this any longer, another piskie with the puffy cheeks of a nut-craving squirrel flew beside her. She would've called him Mesen after an acorn since he looked the part, but she didn't even want to dignify him with a name. He stared at her for a moment, and she groaned.

'Yeah, whaddya want?' she said.

'Um,' he mumbled. 'D-did you tell the g-giant off?'

'Well, maybe. But what good's that gonna do? He's just gonna keep going as always.'

'Ah, th-that's not good,' he stuttered. 'Those humans are getting angrier each day. Just think, if he steps foot in Abmeth, um, well,' he punched the air with a flabby arm, 'I'd t-take him on myself!'

'Yeah, good luck with that.'

He stared at her a moment longer. She wasn't having any more of it.

'Whaddya want?'

'Um, I just want to know, er, why won't you go back to the village?' he asked.

'What's there to do?'

'I mean, it's nice and safe, don't you think?'

'Yup.' She kicked at one of the branch's twigs, snapping it off. 'And also really boring.'

That seemed to silence him. A moment passed, yet he was still there. She hoped he would soon get bored and fly back to Abmeth, but he didn't.

'Is there anything I c-can do to help?'

'Well, I can think of a few things.' Including not talking.

'Ah, well, I, uh..' He trailed off and bunched up closer to her, so close, she felt his breath on her neck.

'Get lost!' She shoved him off of the branch. Shock was written on the annoying piskie's face as his flapping wings kept him airborne. Before he could say anything, however, the giant's footsteps pounded in the distance. Birds whizzed through the air, cawing in terror, and the village soon followed, rushing back to their twig-formed huts. Even that squirrel runt flew back, leaving her on her own at last. To confront a giant once was a suicide mission. To converse with a giant afterwards was a blessing. So, she flew past the many winding roads and felled trees until she reached the dreaded giant. He stared down at the clearing beneath him where clusters of bushes with pink flowers grew. Cormoran's gaze was filled with intent, yet had some sort of yearning to it. The piskie flitted over to him, much to his delight.

'Ah, hello, little piskie.'

'What's goin' on here?' she pressed. 'My village's scared witless 'cause of you.'

'Oh.' He frowned. 'Sorry.'

'Nah, it's fine. They were annoying me anyway.'

'Oh!' he repeated in a happier tone. 'That is quite unusual.' Cormoran looked to the bushes again. 'Can you please do me a favour and pick one of those flowers?'

Her eyes widened. Out of the many things he could've asked, it was rather innocent, but still odd. 'Why?'

'I want to see them up close. I cannot pick them with

these hands.' He made a fist, which could've crushed a boulder if the giant willed it. 'Too big.'

She glanced at him one last time, then shrugged and picked one of the many pink flowers. She wrinkled her nose at its sickly odour, but carried it up to Cormoran regardless, who pointed at his forehead, and she held it in place for him to gaze at. It swayed in the breeze, showing off its many petals and filaments. The giant gave a pleasured chuckle.

'It is beautiful. What is it called?'

'Um,' she said, trying to recall the info from her classes, 'a dog-rose, I think?'

'Dog-rose. Ki-Bryluen. I like the sound of that.'

'It's just a name.'

'Like I said, names give objects their character. It would not be the same if it was only called a common flower. It even has two names.'

'You're a weird thing, aren't ya? I don't get why you're so crazy for names and stuff.'

He let out another chuckle. 'Perhaps I spend too much time pondering such things. But with a lot of time by yourself, you tend to think and digest the information around you. Things you would usually take for granted. Look at the inside of the dog-rose, for instance.'

The piskie snorted, but brought the flower down, staring at its stem, stigma, petals and stamens. All of those parts, however insignificant it seemed, had names attached to them too. That meant they all had to have value. Even she gave the other piskies names, although they were never open to the idea.

'I sorta see what you mean. But hey, aren't we just

waxin' lyrical now? Some fun we're having.'

'How does one wax lyrical?' he asked, picking at his ears. 'Songs do not come from wax.'

That caught her off guard. He was either as dumb as he looked, or was just playing dumb and joking. It stirred something deep in her gut, and she chortled, struggling to keep herself in the air as she tried to contain herself. He let out a guttural laugh in turn, swaying the branches beside them, but neither of them cared. Their laughter soon stopped, and the two gazed at each other for a while. Then, the bushes rustled beneath. They were coming.

'I should be on my way.'

'Wait,' the piskie said, maintaining eye contact. 'I wanna come. Not that we're friends, just that I'm curious.'

Cormoran parted his hair again to uncover his eyes.

'Are you sure?'

'Positive.'

He smiled, walking into the far yonder for the piskie to follow.

Days, weeks, and perhaps a season flew by for the piskie. As she traversed the expansive terrain on outings with the giant, the leaves changed their colours with time. She saw her village less, but the sights glimpsed on her journeys more than made up for it. Starlings raced before their very eyes in murmurations. Sapphire waves crashed against limestone cliffs. Whales danced just below the sea surface. With each moment and conversation shared with the behemoth, from anything about Kernow's history, to the songs the piskie would croon with her group back home, she sensed they had gotten closer as acquaintances. Or maybe even...

Well, perhaps calling him a friend was stretching it. But it was a start.

Yet, for all the time away from the village, its residents often glared at the piskie whenever she got back, noses scrunched up and eyes piercing through her. She tried to ignore it, but the morning after one outing, something happened. When she set foot onto her village's soil, something sloppy and pungent hit her. Squirrel boy grabbed another glob of composted cow pat with a gloved hand, ready to throw again.

'I-I-I know you've laid with the giant; the missus told me so!'

And speak of the devil, the frill-hatted gossip appeared with a group of children who approached the pat pile. This was getting worse, but she knew she had to get out, and at least put up a fight on the way. She grabbed the remaining glob off her forehead and threw it at the runt's face, pelting him in the eye. Score! The children threw more at her in retaliation, but she spun out of the way as her wings elevated her. She stunk, that much was true, but at least there was a place she could wash up, a place she knew he'd be at.

The reservoir near Sed Stedhyans was big enough to house a gargantuan figure such as Cormoran. She settled for something more her size, chose a stream connected to that lake, and left her leafy clothes behind to bathe in the water. She would just fashion herself a new pair once she washed everything off and got moving again. But that could wait; she expected the giant to come around any second now.

Footsteps rumbled the ground, and eventually, Cormoran appeared, dipping his callused feet into the water. He didn't notice her at first, but when she flew over to his brow, he chuckled.

'You are naked,' he said.

'Yeah, and what of it?' she replied. 'My clothes are too small to make much of a difference.'

'Yes, perhaps.' He sniffed the air. 'Did a cow perish nearby?'

'Oh, nay.' She tucked her arms behind her back. 'I got a bit of pat on me, so I've been washing that away.'

'Cow pat?'

'Feh.' She spat to the side. 'Some ass from my village threw it at me, but it's--'

'Because of me? Correct?' His tone was firm.

'Uh, yeah. Not that it matters. I hated his guts to begin with.'

The giant looked down and gingerly lifted his legs out from the lake. He cradled himself, looking like a newborn. 'No matter what I do, everyone seems to suffer because of me.'

'Hey, it can't be helped!' she shouted as loud as her tiny lungs could muster. 'They don't know you! It doesn't matter what they say; idiots will be idiots!'

'And giants will be giants.'

She looked on in stunned silence. He closed his eyes and took a deep breath.

'I suggest you go back to your own village, apologise, and stay there.' He stood up. 'You would be better off without me.'

'H-hey, wait!'

Cormoran walked off, leaving the piskie alone.

She waited until the pounding footsteps were no longer audible. Before she went on her own way, she grabbed a pebble the size of her fist and threw it across the lake. It bounced three times before sinking into the abyss. To think she was becoming friends with the giant. None of the stories with his kind ended happily. Once she realised this, she did not see him for a while. He still hadn't given her a name.

On one particular sunset, the piskie perched atop that familiar branch again. The village burst with activity. Piskies danced in perfect alignment beneath the sunset, flailing burning twigs around them as part of a fire dance in the name of Joan of Wad, wishing each other good fortune. She chose not to join them, even if she had repaired the bond with her own village. It was like every other celebration they held, so it was nothing special. What was the point? But her pointed ears perked up when the piskies chanted yet another name: Cormoran.

'The monster Cormoran will fall!' they sang. 'No longer standing tall! All bless the human Jack! The hunter will attack! Tonight! Tonight!'

Her heart sank at that chant. She jumped off the branch and flew to the island, fearing the worst. Did they find him already? Was there a mob approaching him? Was Jack the Giant Slayer really a force to be reckoned with?

To her relief, Cormoran was still on the island, looming over a small grey rock. It was closer to the coast where it was much easier for someone of his size to be spotted by the humans, but he stood as still as stone with the sandy shore underfoot. When she flew in front of his eyes, they were glassy and glistening in the orange light. They radiated a deep sorrow, so much so that their presence overwhelmed her, and she couldn't bear to look directly at him. Instead, she perched on his shoulder to gaze at the tiny point of interest.

'Er, what's wrong?' she asked.

He sighed so deeply that it vibrated through her body.

'I do not think I told you about her. There was someone else before you that stayed with me, someone of my own kind.'

The piskie tapped her foot on his collarbone.

'What's this about?' she said. 'You know you're in danger, right?'

'Of course. But please, let me tell you quickly.' The giant tilted his huge head towards the mainland. 'She called herself Cormelian. She helped build my place, or should I say, our place, in order to keep our cattle. We lived peacefully for a while, but there was a time when I was less patient.' He made a fist with his other hand. 'Of all things, I was picky about the sort of stones I wanted. White granite, as you see all around you. I didn't even need it; I just wanted to feel like I had control over something.'

He turned his head back to the small rock and sighed again.

'One day, she brought back the wrong stone, and, well, perhaps I lost my temper and kicked her. She just dropped it and left. That was almost a year ago.'

Cormoran ran his hand through the niches of the weathered rock, brushing his fingers against the grooves, then grasped at its entirety.

'The silence. All the days I've spent alone. The one person who filled that void, and now, she's gone.' Another deep sigh. 'I wanted to be as careful as possible after that, especially around you and the humans, but...' He trailed off, resting his chin on his hands. 'They're right to come after me. I am only a mere beast.'

She could neither agree or disagree with that. Instead, the piskie glanced at the mainland where the ocean waves crashed against the stone walls. Clusters of light pricked her vision on the other side. They belonged to torch-wielding humans. The entire causeway leading to the island was laid bare by the low tide. The humans started advancing.

'So,' she said, 'I take it you're not gonna stay here to die.'

'Of course not. Besides, Kernow is too small for me anyway.'

So he would be leaving. To her surprise, hearing that formed a small lump in her heart.

'You know, I've heard all sorts of stories about you folks, and most of 'em ended with the giants gettin' killed or sent away, all because they were bad or something. You don't seem bad at all. It must be a lonely way to live when everyone's afraid you'll eat them.'

'Yes, very much so.' He shut his eyes and clenched his fist before opening them again. 'As much as it pains me, wherever I go, I cannot ask you to come with me. You will bring ruin to your image if you taint yourself with my name.' The giant brought his hand up, laying it flat at the piskie's level to face the sky. 'If you are not afraid, can you stand on my palm? I would like to make one last request.'

Her heart skipped a beat. Considering her size, part

of her felt exposed being in his grasp. Somehow, his aura radiated a sense of calm, so she took a deep breath and flew onto his hand. They gazed at each other, and Cormoran's eyes relaxed.

'I would like you to accept the name Bryluen. Like the dog-rose, it carries a lot of beauty and, without the animal name, it sounds much more elegant, but still wild in nature. What do you think?'

Those words carried a lot of weight even when his voice was but a whisper. She repeated the name to herself, letting it roll off the tongue, and as she did, a warmth spread through the piskie's body.

'It's wonderful,' Bryluen said.

'I'm glad you think so.' Cormoran glanced at the humans on the causeway who had started running towards the island. 'I must take my leave.'

Her mind told her to escape the presence of the approaching humans, but her heart told her it would be the last time she would feel the giant's embrace. She circled her hands around one of Cormoran's fingertips and squeezed it, smiling.

'Well, bye. I hope you find somewhere more your size, Cormoran.'

'And I hope you find your purpose one day, Bryluen.'

She flew off his palm and waved him goodbye as he walked into the ocean. He was waist deep at first, then head deep, and stayed that way, until he was one with the red sky and the ocean surrounding him.

The Teddy Bear's Emporium

by Rachel Fitch

*B*odmin Moor, Cornwall ...
Dora sat in her rocking chair, the only light her fingers worked by was the fiery log fire in the hearth. The wind howled outside and she wondered who or what had tormented the gods this dark night for such a storm to brew. Her fingers worked quickly and steadily, sewing up a lifeless black eye on another unfortunate teddy bear. Another misfit to go on the shelf with the hundreds of others waiting for a home. They were all as ill-favoured as the next one, with their bald patches, misshapen ears and askew eyes; but they had a job to do.

It was quite by accident that Dora became the custodian of the Teddy Bear Emporium. It was on a stormy day, not unlike the storm that was brewing this night, that she stumbled upon the village upon the moor. She had travelled some distance before she had reached here, traversing marshes, roaring rivers, rocky outcrops and the desolate moor itself, all to escape her past of never-ending witch hunts and persecutions. She had nothing but holes in her shoes and a makeshift, felt bag that was perched on her shoulder. A crooked branch, half-burned by lightning, held her stance. If anybody had seen her on that night, they would have come to the same conclusion as those from her past, here stood a witch, but the eyes from this village were already safely tucked up next to their fires and in their beds. They knew how to ride out a storm in these parts.

It had seemed that this was a storm that brings out the spirits. There had been plenty of the lost wandering spirits on the moor but none had bothered her but watched and flittered in her peripheral vision. She noticed, lying in a rain drenched puddle, a hairy rat unmoving and long gone. As she got closer, stifling a choked laugh, she realised it was just a child's teddy bear. One ear and a paw had been chewed, probably by one of the village's true rats. She picked it up and brought it to her chest. That's when the mischievous spirits thought that they would have their fun. Usually she was prepared for such antics but the bear had taken her wits away from her.

A spirit, making use of a swirl of the wind and the energy of a clap of thunder in the night sky, lurched towards her in full terror scream. Its fury and rage cascaded around her in dense fog, soaking her body with rain and making her shiver with cold. Her ears rang with its manic laughter as it swirled around her body causing the fabric of her shawl and her hair to raise to the gods in the sky. Anybody, other than herself - a talker to spirits - would have long since lain motionless in the mud-stained path, their hearts beating no more on this world. More and more spirits entered the melee, pouring out their fury and rage as she stood her ground, not letting them gain what they were wishing: another one of them.

She screamed, not with terror but with her own wrath. How dare they target her? She was not just one of the ordinary folk who lie in their beds, waste their money in public houses, wasting their fleeting lives doing nothing of good upon this earth. She slammed the burned stick in the ground, dropping the forgotten child's bear into the mud. A flash of lightning emitted from the stick, sending sprays of rain water in all directions, the wind blew away from her until she was in her own sense of space. She howled at the ringleader, who came in for another attack. She flung out an arm to stop the gossamer skeleton figure, all teeth and hollow eyes. It staggered until it was held into position by her powerful force. She flung her arm down, sending the spirit downwards. It crashed, not into the path that she was standing on, but into a small furry ball. The teddy bear twitched, a skeleton face tried to squeeze out but it was no good, it was now trapped inside the child's toy.

Dora had since trapped a good sum of the moor's spirits into the misfit bears of hers. She hoped that one day, these bears would find good homes and be once again loved. Then the spirits might find some peace. Since Dora's arrival, the village had experienced good health. Not many of its residents died of heart attacks and such, and it was prospering very well.

Many teddy bears were collected and restored with

odd button eyes, coloured ribbons around their necks, patchwork paws and patched-up ears. They were placed upon the wooden shelves of the cute little shop, with its red and gold front and golden letters that looped and flicked with an artistic touch, on a corner of a little lane. A small wooden donation box would be placed on the counter and a teddy would be picked by an eager child with their pennies clutched in their chubby fists or those tourists eager to take their souvenirs back home. Visitors would tell tales of the strange old woman hunched over in a rocking chair quietly sewing in the corner. Others did not.

The two men in dirty, brown overalls came to sweep up the fallen leaves and the huge tree branch that had damaged the slate roof top after complaints from a number of residents about the eyesore left by the recent storm. They had found the door of the shop unlocked. They entered and turned their noses up at the musty stench and dusty floors where their footprints showed of their existence. One of them leaned on the counter munching loudly on a pasty whilst the other one roughly man-handled the bears before throwing them anywhere on the shelf.

Dora spent the time watching with interest in her corner. She watched as they slap-happily patched up the hole in the roof. She watched as they swept up the odd fallen leaf and then watched with wonder as they bundled teddy bears into boxes. The hours flew by and the scene around her whirled by in a hazed, confused nightmare, until the Teddy Bear Emporium lay still in the emptiness of darkness. Dora scoured the building with heartache. The only things left behind were spiders weaving their webs, a few hungry rats gnawing away within the walls and a small brown furry teddy bear with patchwork ears and a pink bow. Dora hugged the bear to her chest and sobbed until she was resigned to the fact that she was no longer the custodian of the Teddy Bear Emporium. All thoughts of guarding the wandering souls were forgotten. She was no longer needed.

In a tiny village near Bodmin Moor there is a small, red and gold shop. Its golden letters above the door are faded now and its old bay window is covered with a film of grease and cobwebs. Somewhere, amongst the dirt, a small brown furry teddy bear with patchwork ears and a pink bow, twitches with life waiting for that someone to love her ...

Biographies

David Allkins has previously worked for Waterstones and for the charity United Response as a political correspondent. Currently researching various subjects, watching films, reading and struggling with the garden. He can be found on twitter as AllkinsDavid and on instagram as davidallkins

Stephen Baird, after a career in education, is working on a Young Adult historical fantasy set in Renaissance Italy. He published his first novel, *Fire in the Straw*, following a hugely belated gap year. He has also written three plays and a rock musical for 8-13 year-olds. Stephen's wife says her prediction that all three sons would reach adolescence before their dad proved correct. Stephen and Liz live in Truro with their two dogs. Find Stephen on twitter as @sbairdauthor and facebook as Stephen Baird Author

Joshua Copus – Oxland grew up in the South West and has stayed there for most of his life so far. He loves cats and engaging with local arts and writing scenes. Alongside this anthology with the Cornwall Writers, he has also written for publications such as Devon Life and Exploring Exeter. He hopes to release more writing in the future.

TJ Dockree mainly writes fantasy and historical dramas inspired by Cornwall. Her poem, *The Maiden*, won first prize at *Poetry Today – Beyond the Horizon* in 1997. Currently working on three novels: *Timeline 67, Dream Walkers* and *Bait* but by day is editor at *Ethical Rebel* magazine and an ethical fashion and costume designer as *Tracey Dockree* in Truro, Cornwall. www.cornwallwriters.co.uk/t-j-dockree

Ulrike Duran Bravo is German-Chilean and lives in beautiful Cornwall after having travelled and lived all over the world. With an MA in Creative Writing, she has various stories published in anthologies and a short play performed. When not writing, she might be busy teaching, tour-guiding or story-telling. Her favourite days are spent with her two children by the beach.

Froshie Evans is a poet, novelist and screenwriter, which compliments her career in the film industry. She aims to present Cornwall as the diverse and multicultural duchy it is, full of the interesting characters she knows and loves. Froshie is completing a PhD in Cornish Folklore and Digital Culture, and hosts a podcast on the subject entitled "The Celtic Cocktail."

John Evident's fascination with Sci Fi started at 14 with *Rendezvous with Rama* by Arthur C Clark. His favourite author is Anne Mccaffrey. He cannot turn the pages fast enough to read her books as she really captures his imagination. Mccaffrey was the first woman to win a Hugo Award for fiction. John can only dream of reaching such heights. www.cornwallwriters.co.uk/john-evident

Angela Evron lives near the beautiful Perranporth beach which inspired her story. One day at Chapel Rock, she imagined a mermaid sitting there and felt saddened by the destruction of the oceans from plastic waste and its effect on our marine life. She has thoroughly enjoyed developing this idea and is delighted that her story, *Nixie's Quest*, is in this collection.

Rachel Fitch moved from North-East England to Cornwall to develop her career in the education sector, where she spends her time nurturing and caring for the well-being of children throughout Cornwall. When she isn't scribbling down her latest short story, she is creating art and getting crafty ... and the surf is so much warmer down here! www.stardustmagicandeternaldreams.home.blog

Angela Fitt suffers from a thirty-year habit of writing light, lyric verse – usually set to music – for family occasions, folk clubs and social events. She has recently moved into fiction and is loving learning the craft. She'd like to give poignant enjoyment, but will settle for just a half-laugh. www.cornwallwriters.co.uk/angela-fitt

Anita Hunt is Cornish and works in adult social care. With an MA in Creative Writing she is a published poet, theatre reviewer and author. Hobbies include walking her dogs, being crafty and singing with the Rock Choir. When asked how she fits everything in, she shrugs her shoulders, gives you that *I don't know* look and is heard to mutter: 'sleep is for wimps__' She can be found at: www.piskiedreams.com

Pen King lives in a little Cornish village with her husband and collie dog Ben. Her first book, Marmi the Ant, is available in bookshops across Cornwall. Marmi has also made his way to India, America, Israel, South Africa and Australia. It has been said 'These ants are getting all over the place!' Pen can be contacted through the Facebook page for *Marmi the Ant*.

Claudia Loveland gets excited about words and music, and once produced a community musical from twinkle to final curtain. *A Spell in Cornwall* is her first short story. She loves learning new things and seeing other people flourish. Find her at www.cornwallwriters.co.uk/claudia-loveland and on Facebook @ClaudiaLovelandWriter

Emily Charlotte Ould is an enthusiastic lover of country music, cats and books and grew up in Cornwall. She studied Creative Writing at Falmouth University before going on to complete a Masters in Writing for Young People at Bath Spa University. A blogger for Lost in Books, she is also currently seeking publication for her Young Adult novel set in Texas. Find her on twitter as @Lazerbeam_sky

Caroline Palmer has written short stories, novella series, plays and local history series. Now rewriting a 40 year old novel. Wrote, directed and produced two films about John Harris, Cornish poet. The second won Best Documentary at Buxton Film Festival. Enjoys paddling, smelling flowers and gassing with friends and neighbours. FB blogs: The Porthtowan Diary, Caroline Primrose Palmer.

Philip S Rollason is a devoted father, full-time guitar pickup tester and part-time tale spinner from south Cornwall. When he's not staring at a blinking cursor, pondering the horror of said blinking cursor, he can be found on long family walks, lazy beach days, riding down steep things on a push bike (then pushing back up) or playing bass guitar, badly. He can be found on Facebook at Philip S Rollason.

Printed in Great Britain
by Amazon

73409333R00113